DEATH VALLEY SCOTTY

DEATH VALLEY SCOTTY

ROBERT CARTER

ICE BEAR

PUBLISHING

First published in 2014 by Ice Bear Publishing

ISBN-13: 978-1500330071
ISBN-10: 1500330078

Author's Note

This novel is based on a true story. There really was a Death Valley Scotty, and it's worth reminding ourselves that the California that Scotty lived in is only a little over a hundred years out of date.

Today, if you've a mind, you can visit Scotty's Castle. They say it's a great place to ride to if you have a motorcycle. The Castle stands there in Grapevine Canyon much as it ever did, and a lot of people make the trip every year to pay homage to one of California's great characters.

It's always been a puzzle to me that with Hollywood just over the mountains there never was a movie made about Scotty. Now that we have the Coen Brothers, maybe there will be. I hope so.

CHAPTER ONE

Furnace Creek, Death Valley, California

High Summer, 1905

A BEAUTIFULLY DESOLATE desert landscape shimmered in 130 degrees of heat. The ground down here was a cracked salt pan. To the west distant mountains rose up gray-purple. A little nearer, red bluffs, deeply fissured, eroded, guarded the way eastward.

A man with a white hat got down from his mule and wiped his face with his hand. He was looking intently at something in the brightness, blue eyes narrowed. When he pulled a red bandana up over his mouth and nose he looked like he was about to rob a train. But it was only to combat the stink.

The mule he had been riding was leading a second, loaded with gear. Both animals stood amiably in the dusty heat. They were apt to be a little stubborn at times, especially if they were asked to do something they didn't think much of, but they were the right companions for this place, and hardier than any horse.

The man walked around the bodies of two horses lying dead in their traces and bloated by the heat. They had been pulling a four-wheel wagon. As he approached, a mangy black and white sheep dog crept out from the shadow of the wagon. The noise it made was pitiful. It seemed like the dog had survived by licking at the seepage from a water barrel warped by the heat. The dog might have been waiting here four or five days. It was now shaking and crazy with thirst, but its nature remained unthreatening and so he charmed it until it came to him.

"Hey, now, feller. How long you been here?" He unstoppered his canteen and gave the dog a drink of sweet water from his hand. "Who's your master?"

The man finally steeled himself to look up at the body of the dead prospector. He was still sitting up there slouched over on the buckboard like the minute he had died. Only now he was attracting flies.

"Howdy. Weather's a mite warm for this time of year, don't you

7

think?" As he searched the desiccated body the man talked to it as if it was still alive. It made things seem less spooky. "I guess your heart just give out. Happens to a lot of folks who try to get across here."

He found the man's dusty jacket, took out a well-worn blue notebook. In the front was a name, but not a whole lot besides.

"Pleased to meet you Mr. – Jeremiah Wilson," he said, looking up at the discolored face. "Walter E. Scott's the name, but folks call me Scotty, and you can too, if you've a mind."

Scotty set the jacket aside. He'd go through the rest of the pockets when he'd done what he knew he should.

"Say, you wouldn't have a cold beer on you? No? Least you could do for a fellow prospector. I should have asked them in Barstow if they had any grave-digging shovels." He grinned, despite the bad air. "Don't mind me. Just my idea of a little joke. I can see this is going to be one hell of a job."

He unshipped a spade and a pick from the flank of one of his mules and began to bite laboriously into the rock-hard ground ...

A couple of hours later, with the grave dug and filled in again and Mr. Jeremiah Wilson decently sent to his reward, Scotty jabbed the pick and spade back into the ground with finality. He composed himself and addressed the mound of broken earth.

"The Lord is my shepherd; I shall not want," he said. "Yea, though I walk through the Valley of the Shadow of Death, I will fear no evil: for thou art with me. Amen."

It was as much as he could recall.

The jacket wasn't of a quality worth keeping. But one of its pockets might have been worth all the tea in China because it contained a little piece of rock – a very special little piece of rock.

Scotty took off his hat and mopped his brow. "Mr. Wilson, now where in the world did you find *that*?"

It was what they called 'picture rock'. A vein of yellow glittered in it. Scotty turned the rock over this way and that, appreciating the value of what he had found. Then he clasped his hand around it, knowing that he had been well paid for his labor today. A plan was already forming in his mind, a plan to multiply that payment a thousand-fold.

CHAPTER TWO

Chicago, Illinois

THE PLUSH, DIMLY-LIT office of Knickerbocker Trust was all that a cowboy might have expected it to be. Scotty was wearing a white Stetson hat and a blue cowboy shirt, but he had swapped his red bandana for a red necktie. He was a man who respected his surroundings, at least to the extent that whenever he was in a desert he wore a bandana, and whenever he was in a city he wore a necktie. A necktie meant business. The red white and blue theme was on account of the notion that a little patriotism never did any harm where business was concerned.

At the moment, business was sitting across a big desk from him in the person of a rich and suave Chicagoan by the name of James P. Garrett. Rain was beating on the window, a clock was ticking loudly. Garrett's heavy-looking flunky, a man named Doolan, was sitting nearby, picking his teeth but otherwise keeping quiet. A fourth man was in the room, an *expert*: a bald man with spectacles and round collars and the nervous disposition of a bird. The deal was on a knife-edge and Scotty was aware of just how delicate things had become.

Garrett looked again at the picture rock, passed it to his expert, who examined it under a lens and nodded. "Free milling ore. This sample would assay at around two thousand dollars a ton. It's rich, Mr. Garrett."

Garrett sighed. "You heard the man, Mr. Scott. I'm prepared to offer you a grubstake of one thousand dollars to prospect the place you found this."

Scotty produced a pained expression. "It'll take more than a thousand."

Garrett's eyes narrow. "How much more?"

"Five times more."

Garrett blew out a considerable breath. "You'll take one thousand on account."

"Sorry, but I'd need at least two."

"Let's say fifteen hundred, then. You'll take it or leave it, Mr. Scott."

Scotty scratched his jaw like a man who saw the corner he was being pushed into and didn't much like the looks of it. He hesitated, breathed deep, then nodded.

"I still don't think it's enough, but – if I must, I must."

"That's more like it," Garrett smiled, then offered the contract. "Sign here."

Scotty took Garrett's gold fountain pen and signed.

CHAPTER THREE

Los Angeles, Santa Fe Station

THE BIG BALDWIN Ten-wheeler was blowing smoke and steam like an exhausted animal when Scotty got down from the train. He breathed deep, liking the smell of the engine. The power of steam had always put him in awe, never more so than when he walked by a giant black locomotive that had hauled him across half a continent.

The sun was setting in one of those California skies that just go on and on in pastel waves all the way out to Hawaii. Scotty crossed the darkening street and walked a little way Downtown. Not far was his favorite hotel – the Lankershim on 8th, between Broadway and Spring. It was brand new and a touch expensive, but he was still feeling on top of the world. For a split second Scotty wrestled with his conscience, but he easily won. And what does a man do when he feels on top of the world? he asked himself. Right! He celebrates.

He entered the bar where several friends, that is to say a group of men he knew, happened to be gathered together.

"Bartender!" Scotty yelled, and when the bartender, Sam by name, responded, he ordered champagne for everyone.

The group greeted him with slaps on the back and remarks like "Look who it ain't!" and "Well, I never!" and "Where in damnation did you get to?"

And for his part, Scotty told them in his mysterious way that he had been getting up to quite a lot. He had a few secrets that he would not tell – no, sir! But they were welcome to ask him all the questions they liked about his good fortune and his suddenly acquired wealth. The fact was, Scotty had a way of talking that might have been thought of as braggodocio in other people. The dangerous aspect to this charm was that there was just something about him that made people want to believe everything he said.

Pretty soon the group had become convivial and Scotty was laying out fresh twenty dollar bills in buying another bottle and then a third, when who should come in but Warner. Warner was his brother, and with him came a young woman. Now Warner was not at all like Scotty. Two people could not have been less alike, as sometimes happens with brothers, and often leads to wicked rumors and mendacious stories being spread. The truth was: Warner was a worrier. He was wasted away with it. He had thinning hair, a skinny body and a narrow face like someone had stood on his ear as a baby and squashed his head flat sideways. The woman he was with, on the other hand, was sweetly pretty, attractive to a fault, but by the looks of her naturally shy.

She's intimidated by the surroundings, Scotty told himself, thinking it a damned shame that anybody could be intimidated by a hotel bar. But I'll soon bring her out of herself.

"Walter, I got your message. What's this all about?" Warner asked, lowering his voice. "You're not in trouble again, are you?"

Scotty grinned his broadest grin and shook his head and then fell to the task of jocularly admonishing his sibling in a whisper. "Warner, does it *look* like I'm in trouble?" He turned to grin at the young woman "Warner, where's your manners?"

Warner wriggled. There is no other word for it. "Oh. I'm – I'm sorry. Miss Kate Harris – this is my brother, Walter."

"I'm pleased to meet you, Mr. Scott."

"Likewise, Miss Harris. Oh, yes. I hope you're here to help me celebrate? The champagne is on me tonight!"

Warner was all over it like a rash, his little ratty eyes were full of anxiety. "What're we celebrating?"

Scotty took a fresh bottle and popped it. "I just got me a five thousand dollar grubstake. Fifteen hundred of it cash right on the nail!"

Warner blinked. "Keep celebrating like this and you won't have much of a grubstake left."

"Well – you know my motto: easy come, easy go."

"Oh, Walter. Sometimes I just despair of you."

Kate had disengaged herself from the conversation and was staring round at the lamps and the ornate moldings in the ceiling. She didn't look as if she'd wandered into too many bars before, and maybe was wondering what she would do if her mother came by and spotted her through the window. Scotty turned his back on her, leaned toward his brother and muttered "Warner, tell me: are you and she hitched as a team?"

"She's just a friend."

Scotty took the news with obvious pleasure. He turned back to her with a flute glass. "Go ahead. It's all the way from Paris, France. Says right here on the label."

She blinked. "Oh, no. No, thank you, Mr. Scott."

"What's the matter? Don't you like champagne?

"I ... I've never tried it."

"Well, here – find out what you've been missing!"

"Mr. Scott, my job pays twelve dollars fifty a week. I can buy my own drinks if I want to. But thank you all the same."

He liked that. He thought it was an unusual reply, almost a rebuff, and unexpected. But it showed a glimpse of something under her shyness, something that was good and strong and oddly appealing. This was the moment when their eyes really met for the first time, and it seemed to Mr. Walter Scott that he and this girl had hit it off in a way that did not happen all that often.

"Well, good for you, Kate!"

While all this was going on, there was a well-dressed gentleman sitting alone at a table in an unassuming corner of the room. A casual observer might have placed him in his early forties, and might have said of him that he was a no-nonsense sort of feller. He was watching the out-of-focus celebration taking place around the brightly-lit counter. He had been listening for quite a while to the laughter and the expansive storytelling, and tapping a finger on the tabletop every time the word dollar was mentioned. This well-dressed gentleman was busy observing, silently and unsmilingly, as if he had some kind of unstated agenda not unconnected with the man in the red necktie.

Scotty's conversation with Kate was going well. Her reactions had so far shown her to be at least intrigued by him, and possibly a little attracted, although at the same time she seemed somewhat suspicious in a he's-too-good-to-be-true kind of way.

It was hardly surprising. Because Scotty was not exactly holding back. His light was rarely kept under a bushel, but now, helped along by liberal doses of champagne the bushel was nowhere to be seen. "I was the best trick rider Buffalo Bill ever had," he told her. "I can shoot the heart out of an ace at thirty paces. Every time."

"I'm sure you can, Mr. Scott." She seemed less than adequately impressed.

"She don't believe me. Tell her, Warner."

Warner waved his slender hands almost apologetically. "I'm sure she does believe you, don't you Kate?"

"Tell her anyway, Warner."

"That's right. He can."

"I did it most every night for twelve years," he said proudly.

Kate smiled a flat smile. "Riding and shooting hearts out of cards – and now you're a gold miner."

"Owner of the Peerless Mine. That's what I am."

Warner said, "You'd have impressed her more if you'd said you taught school."

"She knows what she's seeing."

Kate nodded. "So where is this ... gold mine of yours?"

"In Hell."

"Oh, that's quite a hard place to mine, I imagine."

"When I say Hell, I mean the hottest place this side of Hell, and the most beautiful this side of Heaven."

"And where's would that be?"

Scotty stuck out a finger and tapped the side of his nose. "That would be for me to know, and for all these other fellers to find out."

CHAPTER FOUR

Chicago, Illinois

TWO WEALTHY MEN were getting off a big steam yacht. It had been a cold day, overcast with iron gray clouds and the kind of moist chill that sweeps off Lake Michigan at certain turns of the season.

They had been out sailing around, taking the air and doing a little light business, but now it looked as if it was about to rain, and so they had called it a day and were looking forward to riding home in their respective automobiles.

One of the men was James P. Garrett, the same we have met with before. The man he was talking with was Albert M. Johnson, a fellow millionaire and President of National Life, one of the biggest insurance companies in the Mid-west.

Although only in his thirties, Johnson walked with sticks towards his waiting Rolls-Royce. He was pale-faced and ill-looking and he was what people called an invalid.

Garrett's sidekick, Doolan, was waiting for him and greeted him respectfully. As Johnson reached the open door of his own car, his chauffeur hovered solicitously, ready to take his sticks.

"So where did he find it?" Johnson said to Garrett.

The other shrugged. "That he doesn't say."

Johnson's face showed his surprise. "So you don't know?"

Garrett shrugged again. "Albert, the man's a cagey operator. He said, that was for him to know and for everyone else to find out."

Johnson nodded. "I can see the logic in that."

"Sure, but I feel like the guy across from me is holding all the aces. I don't like that."

"So what are you going to do?"

"Take a gamble."

Johnson smiled. "If it was my investment I'd watch it a lot closer than you're doing."

"What can I do? I had the sample looked at. What the man showed me was rich ore. If there's as much as he says there is I'm going to end up even richer than you."

Johnson raised a chuckle at that. "Never underestimate the power of insurance, Jimmy. People are scared of getting hurt. Look

15

what happened to me."

As Johnson prepared to get inside his car, his chauffeur leaned forward to help lower him into the big back seat. The millionaire gritted his teeth.

Garrett said, "Think yourself lucky. Not many men come through a broken back."

"Lucky? You're forgetting that my father died in that train wreck."

Garrett took the point, but then produced an open handed gesture. "Well now, if he hadn't you wouldn't be running National Life right now, would you?"

As the car door was closed Johnson sighed, closed his eyes and said, mainly to himself, "No, Jimmy. I wouldn't."

On the seat beside Johnson was a dime novel. The lurid cover showed the romantic figure of a cowboy. The title of the novel was *Shoot Out at Dry Gulch*. When the Rolls-Royce pulled away, he picked it up and turned to the page where he had stopped reading on the way out.

Back at the pier, Garrett's eyes followed Johnson's automobile. He watched a while as it ran along by the lakeside toward the man's North Shore mansion home, then he called Doolan over.

"Mr. Doolan," he said. "I have a little task for you."

"You do, sir?"

"Yes, I do."

CHAPTER FIVE

Death Valley, California

"COME ON, WINDY!"

Scotty called to the dog, and it came to him to lap water from his hand. Every hour, on the hour, that was the way to do it. Windy had been staying at the ironmonger's store in Barstow. She had been treated well and had regained her condition. She had seemed willing enough to follow Scotty back into the desert despite her erstwhile privations.

He took off his red bandana and wiped his face. Digging was always hot work, but those moments when a man looks up from honest toil and sees reality in the raw were rare and beautiful. Death Valley was like that too: the air was clean and there was nobody else to breath it, and the way the light played on the salt pans and the distant mountains was something that fed the soul. His eyes sucked it all in, then he braced his back and got back to digging.

"I could have earned myself five bucks a day shifting earth for the Los Angeles aqueduct," he told the dog. "Now, wouldn't that have been a dumb thing to do?"

As we've already seen, Scotty was no stranger to pick or spade, but here again he was not digging anything up, he was burying. This time the object he was fixing to entomb was a yellow five-gallon kerosene can. There were a dozen more just like it along with two big water barrels in his wagon. The cans were trade marked "Double Zero" and each had two big aughts painted on the side.

For the past two days Scotty had been going from place to place, planting cans in the ground. Every time he set one where he thought it ought to be, he stuck a funnel in the top, then filled it with water, before covering it over and marking it with a little stick with a rag on it.

"Walter's water everywhere," he called out to the clean desert air. "And not any other drop to drink ..."

High up on the red bluffs, way up above the track to the east, a pair of field glasses were tracking Walter Scott as he urged his mules along. A sheepdog was trotting along beside him in a land woefully devoid of sheep, and woefully full of heat haze. Everything shimmered like boiling mercury and Doolan squinted because of the salt sweat that kept picking the corners of his eyes and misting up the lenses they were trying so hard to peer through.

What was happening below remained a mystery to Doolan. He sweated and sweltered to no avail whatsoever. When he had first started it had seemed like a simple mission: to follow a cowboy to his gold mine and then to return in triumph to his boss and report on the matter. For two days he had stuck at his task and now he was all but out of provisions and nursing only enough water to make it back to the pass through which he had entered this God-forsaken land. Now he was dressed in rough desert clothes and lying low in a hollow, watching at intervals, and wiping his eyes the rest of the time. The rocks he was sitting on were sharp and hot enough to fry eggs. The skin on his face had peeled, his lips were dry and he was covered in dust. He got up, brushed his mouth against the back of his hand and spat.

"To hell with him," he said to the empty air. "I've had just about enough of this!"

CHAPTER SIX

Los Angeles, California

DOOLAN, NOW DRESSED in a tight city suit looked up from his newspaper and his eyes narrowed with recognition. He had spotted his quarry as the man headed towards his favorite Los Angeles hotel – and his favorite Los Angeles hotel bar.

Doolan had got back to Barstow two nights before, wholly out of water and on his last legs. The burns on his desert-ravaged face had yielded somewhat to Mrs Jessop's chamomile lotion. The Barstow druggist's wife had fussed over him for a full half hour before she had let him go board his train.

"Didn't anybody tell you how dangerous Death Valley is?" she had asked him. "You didn't think maybe that's how it got its name? What you want to go down there for anyhow?"

All things considered, he'd wished that she would mind her own business.

Doolan gave it five minutes, checked his pocket watch and decided it was about time to go in. He sidled into the bar and found himself a quiet place to sit down.

In the bar, all was good cheer. Scotty was hailed by his usual group of bar flies. Warner and Kate were already there, and the evening was all set to roll. Scotty began by cracking a few jokes and pretty soon the group were standing around him, roaring with laughter. He was plying them with free drinks and being conspicuously generous. He gave a big tip to the barman and a silver dollar to the paper boy who had learned to sneak in to sell him a copy of the *Examiner*.

"Have you really got a secret gold mine in Death Valley, Mr. Scott?" the kid asked.

The boy was immediately collared by the Swedish lobby manager. "Out!"

"Hey, Lars, put him down! He ain't no ringtail. That's my good friend Danny Mayer. He's the first one I ever told about the Peerless Mine."

"This is yoost a no-good kid! He got no business in here. I tole him dat."

"Careful with him! He's gonna own the '*Examiner*' someday, ain'tcha, Danny?"

Danny yelled back from under the Swede's arm. "You bet, Mr. Scott!"

Kate was watching Scotty's joking with a strange fascination. Ordinarily she had a short way with any kind of showing off, but in Scotty's case she couldn't help herself. There was a spark in her that responded to Scotty's brand of showmanship. She had never seen anything like him before. He knew exactly how to make himself the center of attention, and he liked being there. He would have been magnetic at ten paces – right up close he was positively mesmeric.

"What's a ringtail?" she asked Warner.

"I guess it's his word for a scoundrel. That is to say, an untrustworthy person."

"I suppose spending too much time in the desert has a peculiar effect on a man."

Warner sighed. "Yes. It usually makes a man crazy."

"But I don't think your brother's crazy." A moment of doubt assailed her. "Is he?"

Warner sighed again. "I am often driven to wonder about that."

But crazy or not, Kate was captivated and without any kind of defense. She had been brought up to have her feet firmly planted on the ground and to keep them there, but some part of her liked the idea of being swept away. She was like a person standing on the edge of a cliff resisting that feeling that comes over some people to throw themselves over.

"Hey, come on over here, Kate ..."

She came. She was demure and reluctant, but she came.

"Look! I got this for you."

He took out an atomizer bottle of perfume, and Kate was taken by surprise. She didn't get many gifts. Scotty relished her delight, the look that flitted across her face before she remembered herself and guarded her face. He sprayed a little perfume on the back of her hand, raises her hand to his nose, sniffed with a rapturous expression on his face. When he opened his eyes he was looking straight into hers. And she was looking straight into his.

"*Belle de Nuit*," he said. "That's French for 'Beauty of the Night'."

20

Kate reddened with embarrassment. "Walter, you shouldn't have."

"Why not?"

"Wasn't it bought out of your grubstake money?"

He looked left and right confidentially, then put his mouth close by her ear. "You better enjoy that bottle," he murmured. "Because it was bought with the very last nickel of it."

There was shock in Kate's eyes. The kind of shock that anyone could have kept spending so steadily on luxuries that all of fifteen hundred dollars had been gotten through. She recoiled from the idea. How could she enjoy a bottle of perfume knowing what she did? It would be tantamount to enjoying stolen goods.

"Don't worry," Scotty said, winking at her. "There's more where that came from. All I have to do it wire for it."

She sniffed at her hand. Despite all her misgivings, it still smelled wonderful.

Scotty yelled at the bar. "Sammy! Another round of drinks for my good friends if you please!"

"Coming right up, Mr. Scott."

But before Scotty could turn around again a couple of strangers had approached. The first man was tall and blond and handsome in a way that was probably attractive to women. The other was not.

"Say, now, Mr. Scott," the blond stranger said. "You ever thought about investing your profits in mining stock?"

Scotty gave the idea scant credit. "Sounds to me that would be like putting my gold right back in the earth again."

Everyone laughed at the quip, but undeterred the blond man offered his hand. "Z. Beldon Gaylord, how are you, sir?"

"Well, I guess I'm about as happy as a butcher's dog, Zee."

More peals of laughter rang out as Gaylord passed over his calling card. "It just so happens that I may have a little business proposition for you."

"Is that so?" Scotty grinned back. "If I had a dollar for every time I heard that, I'd be exactly *half* as rich as I am now."

Everyone else found that uproariously funny, but Gaylord declined to laugh. Perhaps, Scotty thought, he wasn't drunk enough yet.

"Think that remark through, Zee. You'll find it's worth the

21

effort."

"Please, call me Beldon," Gaylord said quickly pressing on. He pulled over the other man. "May I introduce a friend of mine?" This here is Frank Sanders, editor of the *Los Angeles Examiner*."

Frank Sanders was a middle-aged man. Unattractive on account of an unfortunate arrangement of facial features, but he was clearly no fool. He'd been appraising Scott ever since the two of them had walked in, a fact far from lost on the subject of the appraisal.

"It's a pleasure to meet you, Mr. Scott," Sanders said.

Scotty took the hand that was offered. "Howdy-do. Always glad to make the acquaintance of a gentleman of the press." He raised his glass in a toast. "Here's to you as good as you are. And here's to me as bad as I am. But as good as you are, and as bad as I am, I'm as good as you are, as bad as I am!"

Sanders seemed unwilling to work out if that was an insult or a compliment, but he took it as the latter anyhow, which showed the caliber of the man.

"And the same to you, Mr. Scott," Sanders said, raising his newly-filled glass.

"An Irish feller once taught me that toast," Scotty said with a grin, turning his attention back on the crowd he had been momentarily neglecting. "Now, did I ever tell you folks about how I first come across the Peerless Mine ...?"

Sanders moved away and went to sit at a table in an unassuming corner of the room. It was the same unassuming corner where a no-nonsense gentleman in his early forties had sat, working on an agenda while listening to Scotty's entertaining badinage some weeks before. The same man was here again, and he greeted Sanders as a magnate greets a minion.

Scotty's voice rose up above the general din. "Did I ever tell you about the time when I got snake bit? Rattlesnake it was. Damned thing was as big as the last Republican majority. Six foot if it was an inch, and fangs on it like a Mexican's spurs ..."

"This man Scott is pure gold," the magnate said.

"Did you say gold, sir?"

"Oh, yes. Fool's gold maybe. But stick with him, Sanders. His kind sells newspapers."

The minion nodded in thoughtful agreement, then said, "Yes, sir. I will, Mr. Hearst."

CHAPTER SEVEN

Chicago, Illinois

JAMES P. GARRETT WAS sitting alone with Doolan in his plush Chicago office. Dark mahogany paneling, a huge desktop in gilded green leather and a swiveling chair that made a man look like a boss and, what was even more important, feel like one. But he was not a happy boss.

A dim northern blue-white light was filtering in through the tall windows. It was wet weather again outside. Doolan was nervous, his face incongruous in the inclement weather, it being still sun-blasted and peeling. He had a small, red notebook in his hand.

Garrett was flinty-eyed. "So?" he said with all the brevity he could muster.

Doolan shook his head. "I just couldn't figure it at all, sir. If Scott's prospecting he has a strange way of doing it."

Garrett waited for Doolan to go on.

"Sir, he just rode around the Valley all day in 120 degrees of heat, digging holes and burying kerosene cans. Jesus – the man's got to have an asbestos hide."

Garrett's flinty eyes blinked. "Burying *kerosene* cans, you say?"

"I swear to you, sir," Doolan said. "That's all he did."

"Scott must be fixing to *burn* the gold out."

Garrett's sarcasm only added to Doolan's discomfort. "It was all I ever saw him do. That and fix ham and eggs twice a day. He had a mutt with him too. A black and white one."

"Great work. Mr. Doolan. Amazing detail you managed to record," Garrett said barely controlling himself. "Maybe he's training the dog to sniff out the gold."

Doolan eyed his employer with a sidelong glance. "I'm sorry, sir, if it's not what you wanted to hear. It's just – that's what he did."

Garrett felt like he had handed out a job and it had come winging straight back at him like a flying machine. He looked accusingly at Doolan. "How long did you follow him?"

"Days and days, sir. I lost track. In all, maybe ... ten, eleven."

Garrett's stare hardened. "You've been away a *month*, Doolan."

"Yes, sir. But a month in that place would be beyond human

endurance." His eyes glazed. "Sir, I can't describe it to you. Time has no meaning out there. It's a wilderness, desolate and burning, like ... Hell itself."

Garrett showed no sympathy. "Doolan I sometimes wonder what on earth I pay you for."

The other hung his head.

"All right, let's go over it from the beginning." Garrett drew breath. "Where'd he go when he left Death Valley?"

"Sir, straight back to Barstow – to stable his mules."

"You mean *my* mules."

"Yes, sir. Your mules. After that he caught the train to Los Angeles." Doolan offered the red notebook. "I made a list here of all the restaurants he ate at – they're all expensive joints, Mr. Garrett. The hotel, the bars. He's quite a drinker. And he has a lot of friends who are drinkers too."

Garrett was angry now. He brushed the notebook aside. Slapping the back of his hand against one of Scotty's begging letters. "He's had the audacity to write me for another five hundred bucks and sent me his IOU for a thousand." He fixed Doolan with a hard look. "You're telling me I've been taken for a ride, aren't you, Mr. Doolan?"

"I don't know what else to think, sir."

"And that means I've been a fool?"

This time Doolan stayed silent.

"*Am* I a fool, Mr. Doolan?"

Doolan looked down uncomfortably. "No, sir."

"Good. because the day you think I'm a fool is the day you'll start looking for another employer. Now get out of my sight."

As Doolan left, Garrett opened his desk drawer, took out a telegraph message blank and began to write on it.

Across town, Albert Johnson was at home in his mansion. His library was a room designed to inspire awe – dozens of shelves, thousands of classic books all with gilded spines, a library two floors high, complete with a spiral stair, an acre of wood paneling and a huge, stained glass ceiling.

It was raining hard outside, and the usually magnificent view across the lake was a watery grey blur. Johnson was sitting glumly

25

on his couch, propped on cushions with a plaid rug over his legs. The pulp dime novel he was reading was called *A Town Called Vengeance*. There was a lurid western scene on the front cover, Joshua trees and all.

Johnson let the book fall as he began to cough painfully. As if on cue, his nurse, Margaret, appeared with his medicine.

"Now, Mr. Johnson. This will ease your chest. It'll stop your wheezing too. Open wide."

He did as he was told and she fed him a spoonful of the evil-looking green medication. He made a face just as his wife, Bessie came in to see that he was comfortable. She fussed around him for a moment.

"The Lord knows how you suffer, Albert, my dear."

"That's a great comfort to me, Bessie."

She leaned over and gave him a chaste peck on the forehead. "There, there. I told you not to exert yourself."

"I hope they have Appaloosas in the Kingdom to come," he told her. "You know that would be my idea of Heaven."

"Appaloosas?" she said. "What on earth are they?"

Johnson's eyes sparkled. "Injun hosses!"

"Oh, Albert," Bessie said chiding him gently. "So many wonderful books in here, and you will fill your head with all that cowboy nonsense. Let me plump your pillow for you."

As Bessie left, Arthur, the family's lugubrious butler arrived. He brought the evening paper, the *Chicago American*, up to Albert. He bowed forward from the waist and stuck out a silver platter on which the paper rested. It had been flat-ironed to remove unnecessary creases.

"Thank you, Arthur."

"A pleasure, sir," the butler said bleakly and retired.

The headline read:

OWNER OF THE PEERLESS MINE
CLAIMS TO HAVE BEEN ROBBED
OF $12,000 IN GOLD DUST
ON THE SANTA FE TRAIN ROBBERY BETWEEN
FORT MADISON AND GALESBURG

Johnson reached back to the small table where an ornate telephone instrument stood. He picked it up and rang the exchange.

"Hello? Give me Michigan 207."

While he waited for the connection, Johnson felt a certain excitement gathering inside him. "Ah, hello Mr. Doolan. No, it's not Mr. Garrett I want to talk to, it's you. Yes. It's about what you told my driver about finding a new job. You know, I might have just the position you're looking for."

Scotty stood facing Garrett in the latter's office. He had expected to be asked to sit down, and when no invitation came he did it anyway.

Garrett's sidekick, Doolan, came into the room through a frosted glass door and stayed by it, looking on from a distance.

Scotty shook his head innocently. "You wanted proof, Garrett, so I was bringing you proof. First fruits of the Peerless Mine."

"You want me to believe that twelve thousand dollars' worth of gold dust was stolen from the train? That you just let someone take it away from you like that?"

"There it is, right there in black and white. Don't you believe what you read in the papers?"

"You must think I'm a fool – "

Scotty shrugged. "Aw, I'm not greatly worried about it. It's just a sample. Twelve thousand bucks worth is about as much as a man can carry without straining himself. I got drunk and some ringtail took it. So what? I'll go back get some more. A thousand bucks should cover the costs."

Garrett seemed to be suppressing strong emotions. "You know what I think? I think you're a liar and a fraud. I know you didn't do any prospecting. I had you followed."

Scotty cast a glance at Doolan and snickered. "Sure you did. Think I didn't see Mr. Ringtail, here? Every time he crossed a ridge there he was big as a building. Setting up there watching me with those big ol' field glasses glinting away like signal mirrors in the sun."

Garrett shot an accusing glance at Doolan.

Scotty chuckled, sat way back in his chair and pushed up the brim of his hat with his forefinger. "If there's one thing I wasn't ever about to do it's signpost a trail to the Peerless Mine."

"*Our* mine." Garrett reminded him.

"My mine," Scotty corrected. "According to our contract half the gold in it belongs to you, but the mine ... is mine."

Now, James P. Garrett regarded himself as a man of business: practical, level-headed, even hard-bitten if it came to it. But as he stared at the openest expression ever to show on a man's face his mind went blank. In that moment he could think of nothing at all to say.

"Look," Scotty told him by way of filling the vacuum. "Just give me fifteen hundred bucks and I'll leave right this minute. I'll fetch you back another sample. I can be here again in thirty days. Now is that fair? Or is that fair?"

The sun had set and a bright half moon was riding high in the south, silvering field and tree alike. Harry Boyce, the uniformed driver of James P. Garratt's expensive automobile, had figured out long ago that an easy life may be had by any man if only he could find and keep a good job. Harry Boyce had found his own good job and he had kept it five years. He knew that, in large part, that happy state was due to his observing the Golden Rule: a willingness to do as he was told and not inquire into matters that did not directly concern him.

He was separated from his two passengers by a glass screen. The two men in question sat side by side on the back seat: Doolan on the right, and Doolan's unwilling guest on the left. A white ten-gallon hat sat in the space between them.

Both men were silent, both were looking out the windows in opposite directions, and wearing equally bored expressions as the darkness slid by. Had Harry Boyce wanted to, he could have looked over his shoulder. And if he had, he would have seen Doolan's hand holding the butt of a big revolver whose business end was pointed straight at the other man's belt buckle.

But Harry Boyce wasn't about to break his Golden Rule.

The drive had taken them out through the city of Chicago, past the shacks and tenements of the West Town and an hour further down the dusty road into a darkening sunset. After they had crossed a large river bridge the car took a right and bounced along a rutted track for a while, past what looked like a derelict saw mill. It drew

28

up in a yard a little way from a couple of sheds that stood at right angles to one another.

Harry Boyce stayed inside the car while the passenger got out, followed by a very matter-of-fact Doolan. He looked the other way when Doolan marched the man round the back of the left-hand shed, and kept going until they were out of sight of the car. Harry Boyce watched moths dancing in the headlights. His fingers tapped the wheel as he contemplated getting out his tobacco and rolling a cigarette. Then a sudden noise made him flinch. It didn't matter that he was expecting it. It didn't matter that it was the sound of a handgun being fired.

Ten seconds later Doolan walked across the beam of the headlights and got back inside the car. He made no comment, except to say one word: "Home."

"Yes, sir, Mr. Doolan."

The car turned a broad circle and drove off back the way it had come. As it motored away, a white ten gallon hat flew out the window and landed in a pile of moldering sawdust.

It didn't take a genius to figure out what must have happened to the other passenger, but Harry Boyce was a man constitutionally inclined to steer away from all difficulties. And he steered away from this one.

In back of the shed, Scotty watched thoughtfully as blue gunsmoke haze slowly dissipating in the moonlight. He listened as the car rolled away, and once silence descended he got up, struck a match and looked thoughtfully at the bullet hole in the shed door. It was a fair size – he could poke two fingers clean through.

A second match revealed the business card that Doolan had put into his hand before leaving. The address on it said:

Albert M. Johnson,
21115 Devonshire Blvd,
North Shore, Chicago. Il.

He turned it over. In educated handwriting it said:

8 p.m., Tuesday

"Be there," had been Doolan's only remark. Doolan, being a man of comparatively few words at the best of times, had made it sound much more like an order than an invitation.

That, Scotty decided, was definitely food for thought.

Night had blackened the tall windows of Albert Johnson's impressive library. Johnson himself was watching with rapt attention, looking up as his guest talked. The latter was sitting on top of a stepladder, the one that would have been used to reach the higher books had anyone ever troubled to search for one.

Now the stepladder had a western saddle on it. It was, so to speak, a wooden horse, and Scotty was aboard it. He was wearing his usual white ten gallon hat and his red bandana was round his neck. He had on a pair of sheepskin chaps and a low-slung gun belt too. From his holster he drew a revolver and twirled it impressively.

"And that's how the Old Glory Blowout come to be Buffalo Bill Cody's first success. It was the first rodeo! Ain't nobody could shoot like me. I'm telling you flat."

Johnson's excited eyes glowed. "What did you use?"

Scotty roared. "Why, a Peacemaker. What else?"

Johnson's fists clenched and he beat the air. "I knew it! I knew it! Can you still do it like you used to?"

"I'm a mite rusty, and it ain't the same as at the gallop, but sure I can!"

Johnson, flushed with enthusiasm, pulled a treasured possession out of his desk drawer, walked up to the stepladder and offered up the hand gun like it was a holy relic.

"See this?" he said. "Plated. Pearl handled. Engraved by Eli Whitney Jr. himself! One in ten thousand. Be careful, it's loaded."

"It better be." Scotty hefted the Colt and felt the balance. "Oh, now *that* is what I call a very a fine weapon."

Johnson, enraptured by the spirit of the moment, rose up inside himself and demanded, "See that damned skylight? It's been frowning down on me for ten years and I *hate* it! Put six shots through that boss angel, Mr. Scott – if you can!

"If I can?" Scotty scoffed.

Twenty-five feet above them the 'skylight' in question over-

30

arched the library with six priceless panes of stained glass. Angels and cherubim struggled with one another in a dozen unlikely poses. They had been brought over specially from some famous colored glass factory in Paris, France.

Very rapidly, one after another, the boss angel's various parts shattered in a shower of broken glass.

"Yay!" Johnson yelled ecstatically.

"Yahoo!" Scotty hooted.

"Waaaaa!" cried Bessie.

Both men turned like naughty schoolboys caught in the commissioning of some nefarious act.

Johnson's wife stood aghast in the open double doorway, clutching her big black Bible to her chest. Bessie's vocal distress had put a very sudden end to their game of cowboys.

When they looked back at her, she was the very picture of a person overcome by amazement and horror. Worse still, she had been joined by her two confederates: on the one side was Johnson's nurse, while on the other stood the unflappable butler. None of them were amused.

Johnson, suddenly sober and solicitous, said, "Bessie, I can explain."

Bessie said only, "Albert?"

Scotty, wisely, said nothing at all.

Albert smiled at his wife in an I-can-explain kind of way, but then his wife said, "Albert ... You're walking ... You're walking without your sticks!"

Albert looked back almost apologetically, then looked to Scotty.

"Yaaaaa-hoooo!"

CHAPTER EIGHT

Los Angeles, California

TONIGHT, SCOTTY WAS surrounded by an even larger crowd than usual. Kate was there and Warner was there, and all the regular faces seemed to have brought along an eager acquaintance. The champagne was flowing again, and Scotty was spending liberally.

"Yes, sir," he told them all loudly. "I got pay dirt that'll assay in at ten thousand dollars a ton!"

That drew gasps of amazement, and toasts to his great good fortune.

Beside him, Kate was holding up a copy of the *Examiner*. It told the tale of the train robbery in intricate and absorbing detail. "They're saying it's made the front page of every paper in the country. Warner was so worried for you."

"Warner? Worried, you say?" He smiled at her. "Hmmm, you smell so good tonight."

Kate scowled prettily. "Scotty he really was, and so was I."

"Why, Warner's always worried. If he wasn't worried, he'd be worried about why he wasn't. Warner enjoys worry, don't you, Warner?

Warner, sick-faced, whispered an attempt at an aside. "Where did you get the money from this time?"

"I ran off my old backers," Scotty said out the side of his mouth. "Got tired of their dumb questions so I changed them for more deserving ones."

"More stupid ones, you mean. Walter, don't you realize what -"

Scotty raised his voice to address his admirers, "Yes, sir, the Peerless Mine is the richest mine in all the Americas. You can write that down, Mr. Sanders. There's two t's in Scotty, by the way."

Nearby Z. Beldon Gaylord shot a shrewd glance at Sanders, then said, "You lost a lot of money on that train to Chicago."

Scotty laughed. "Seventy-two hours is a long time for a man to stay on guard."

Warner tugged at his sleeve. "Walter, I need to talk with you."

Gaylord, always ready with a plausible proposition, said, "I may be able to help you make it back. The general manager of the Santa

Fe Railroad Company is a very good friend of mine."

Scotty's ears pricked at the information. "Is that a fact, Zee? – Warner, just a minute willya? – But, Zee, twelve thousand bucks?" He snapped his fingers. "Who cares about that? I wouldn't get out of bed for it."

Warner eventually succeeded in pulling him round. "God help me! Will you listen?" He turned to the others and said acidly, "Excuse us just a moment."

Scotty rolled his eyes and allowed himself to be pulled out of earshot.

Warner's whisper was fierce. "Where did you get the money?"

Scotty, still jovial, but his patience beginning to wear thin, said, "What are you, Warner? Your brother's keeper?

"What did Garrett say?"

"About what?"

"For god's sakes – about the train robbery! About his grubstake!"

Scotty put on an indulgent expression. "Don't worry about Garrett."

"And what happens when they come looking for you?"

"Nobody will come looking for me. Will you, for once in your life, just try to relax?"

"What happens when Garratt's boys come looking for you, and they find *me*? Or Kate? Have you thought about that?"

"That won't happen." Scotty's mouth broke into an unstoppable grin. "Garrett thinks I'm dead."

Warner was appalled. "*What?*"

"Listen, it's his loss. The man never did have any faith."

Warner was intensely worried now, at least three shades of worry more electric than was usual. "Walter! Where did you get the goddamned money? Pulleeeeze!"

Scotty recognized his brother's state and sighed. "Warner ... will you quit?" He lowered his voice. "I got me a much bigger backer than Jimmy Garrett ever was."

"Who?"

"His name's Albert M. Johnson. He owns National Life Insurance Company, the biggest firm west of the Mississippi. He's just bought himself 50% of the Peerless Mine. Hey, ever see a portrait of General Meade?"

"What?"

Scotty unbuttoned the left breast pocket of his shirt and took out five likenesses of General Meade. They were – every single one of them – $1,000 bills.

Warner almost fainted with dismay. "Oh, God!" he begged. "Please, God in heaven, tell me this is *not* happening."

CHAPTER NINE

"Camp Holdout," Death Valley

A WEEK AGO Scotty had been glad to be back in his desert, but after seven days he had begun to feel he had had his fill of oven heat for the moment. He knew he had to spend time here, and do all the things people expected of him, so he had bent his mind to building a base of operations to make life a little more pleasant.

But it had been hot work. He breathed deep. Sunset was a good time of day here. For the last half hour he had been making hot cakes in his skillet at "Camp Holdout" and taking care with the cuisine. The camp was in fact a small cave, a kind of cleft in the rock, but now there was a name shingle up on a pole and a piece of dusty canvas rigged up outside as a sunshade for the mules. Inside was a store of water barrels, food, fodder, tools and all the other provisions a grubstake ought to buy. Scotty's rifle – a Mauser '98 – was propped up beside him.

Windy watched him as expectantly as sheep dogs always do, ready at a moment's notice to herd any sheep that might just happen to appear. Scotty's own eyes however were on the great orange disc of the sun as it settled behind Telescope Peak.

"There's *got* to be gold here," he told the dog. "Someplace."

Los Angeles, California

Scotty sat with Kate in a fancy restaurant, a *very* fancy restaurant. It was large and seated plenty of other well-dressed diners. Scotty and Kate were chowing down a good meal. Kate was smiling, but she seemed uncomfortable about something.

She said, "Scotty, would you mind taking your hat off since we're at table?"

Scotty regarded her idea with muted enthusiasm. "What for?" he asked.

"Manners."

"Kate, this here is my trademark. If I take it off how're folks going to recognize me?"

"Is that why you always dress the same? So folks will recognize you? White hat, blue shirt, red necktie?"

"I can't think of a better color scheme. Beats carrying around two or three different kinds of clothes."

"But I never see you wear anything other than a red necktie. Why is that?"

"What would you have me wear? A red shirt, a blue hat and a white necktie? I reckon that would make me look too much like a bandit."

Kate looked at him closely. "Is that what you are, Scotty? A bandit?"

"I like to come down to one of these fly-up-the-creek kind of places now and again, don't you? Just to prove I can do it with the best of them."

But Kate wouldn't let him off the hook. She latched onto his eyes and got serious. "Tell me, Scotty. Are you for *real*?

Scotty traded her, candid eye for candid eye. "Kate, I am a *rich* man. And that is a fact."

"That's not what I asked you. I said, are you for real?"

He nodded. "Yes," he said. "I *am* for real."

Kate smiles, vastly glad to hear him make that kind of flat out promise. "Good," she said. "Only, I'm not sure I could stand it if I found out you weren't."

As Scotty looked at her he understood that she wasn't interested in how rich he was, she was interested in how *genuine*. It seemed to him that that she was on the edge of a big decision about him, and that was not only humbling it was something that needed a little steering.

"See," he said. "The trouble with you, Kate, is you don't have no judgment of other people."

Kate sat back, feeling possibly insulted. "Well, I like that!"

"Don't get me wrong," he said, making light of it. "But it's true. You wouldn't know a millionaire if one stood right there in front of you."

"What makes you say that?"

"Because it takes one to know one."

She put down her knife and fork. "Well, I bet I could tell a millionaire just as well as you can."

"Oh, yeah?"

"Yeah!"

36

Scotty put his knife and fork down too. "All right, show me. Who's the only other millionaire in here tonight?"

Kate narrowed her eyes as if it was a trick. Her eyes went around the room as she tried to decide who it might be. There was a middle-aged couple by the pillar who might fit the bill, another by the potted palms. Finally she pointed to a well-dressed man dining with a younger friend.

"Him. Right there."

Scotty looked to where a pair of bespectacled men in vest suits ate with pronounced good manners.

Scotty gave a private smile. "Nothing but a bank president and his friend from out of town. Try again."

Kate's glance was suspicious. "How do you know?"

"By the way his eyes are dead behind those little round lenses, and that fancy suit of clothes he's wearing."

"They both look pretty well-dressed to me."

Scotty shook his head. "That's where you're wrong. See, real millionaires don't ever dress like that. They don't want folks to know who they are."

Kate laughed. "Well, *you* do!"

"Ah, but I'm different. I got a reppertation to keep up."

Kate's patience wore out. "So who is it?"

"Who's what?"

"Who's the other millionaire in here?"

"Oh ... that." He didn't quite break out into a smile. "You see that feller over there?"

She watched him toss his head to his left to where an old, shabbily-dressed man was sitting alone in the corner of the room, shoveling down food from an upturned fork like he hadn't eaten in months. She looked at him with an unconvinced expression.

"Him? In the corner? I don't *believe* you!"

"I'm telling you. He's the other millionaire in this place. Name of Bill."

"Not a chance!"

Scotty sighed, as innocent eyebrows lifted. "Straight as an arrow. Watch." He made a piercing two-finger whistle then shouted across the room. "Hey, Bill!"

The diners fall silent, turned to see what the rude commotion was about. Kate, hugely embarrassed, suddenly wished she was in an adjoining state. "Oh, Scotty, please ..."

The old man waved back with a toothless grin.

"See?" Scotty said amiably. "That's Bill, all right."

Despite her embarrassment, Kate managed to say, "That doesn't prove anything!"

Scotty shouted again. "Hey, Bill! Come over here a second, willya?"

Again all conversation died. All the other diners were trying hard to look as if they were not watching, but they were.

Kate's cheeks had gone so far as to actually redden. "Scotty, everyone's looking at us."

"Let 'em look. They ain't nobody."

Bill's chair was in the middle of being scraped back. The old man got unsteadily to his feet and came over to join them.

"How ya doing, Scotty?" he said.

"I'm just fine, and hoping you are the same. But here's a thing, Bill: you know, I find myself a little short today. How about lending me a coupla bucks?"

Bill grinned merrily. "Sure, Scotty! For you, anything, anytime, you know that. Here ya go."

He fished in his pocket and took out a dollar and slapped it on the table. It looked like a dollar, except on closer inspection, Kate saw there was a portrait of General Meade on it.

"That enough for you, Scotty?" Bill winked and tapped the side of his nose. "Want to take another? Just in case?"

"Why, that's generous of you, Bill. But, no. I guess this will have to see me through tonight. I appreciate it."

"Don't mention it."

Bill went back to his dinner. Kate's face was still registering speechless amazement as Scotty started to eat.

"What?" Scotty smiled. "You know Bill ain't his real name. I just call him that 'cuz he's always good for a dollar."

Los Angeles, California

A uniformed policeman was controlling the traffic at a busy downtown road intersection as Scotty dodged horse drawn vehicles and automobiles alike to reach the sidewalk. He looked up gratefully at First Pacific bank, then down at his watch, thinking that it would be a shame to be late, but on the other hand it would be worse to get run over on a day as important as this.

Once inside the crowded banking hall he took a moment to look around: judging by the grand interior, banking seemed to be a profitable line of work. It looked to Scotty like the business could spare a little money if push ever came to shove. A number of young men appeared, ready to ask questions and take written notes. They were reporters who had been sent on a tip-off to cover the great event.

Scotty forestalled the clamor with a raised hand. "Stick around, boys. First things first. Business calls."

Out of a door marked 'W.G. Fullerton, President', the head man emerged to give his client the red-carpet treatment. Scotty smiled as he recognized the same man who had been in the restaurant three days ago, the one whom Kate had mistaken for a millionaire.

It seemed that everybody on the bank staff had been waiting for Scotty's arrival, because there was a buzz of expectation in the air, and everyone turned to watch as he raised his hat at the banker.

"Oh, Mr. Scott, we're very pleased you made the wise decision to bank with First Pacific."

"This place is mighty convenient – real close to my favorite drinks bar."

A ripple of amusement passed among the spectators as Fullerton indicated the frosted glass door of his office. "Please, step inside, won't you?"

As Scotty went in he turned to the reporters, "I'll be out in a little while, boys. Don't go away now." Then he called after Fullerton "I want me a bank account with a check book and regular interest paid on the nail, just like we agreed across the telephone ..."

The door closed and Scotty sat down.

"I don't believe that will be a problem, Mr. Scott. We always have special checkbooks made up for all our premium depositors." He indicated a number of items on his desk blotter. "See here, your name printed in gold on a genuine crocodile skin checkbook cover. And a special gold-nibbed Waterman fountain pen with First Pacific and your name engraved on it."

Scotty grinned as he examined the pen. "I get a lot of firms wanting me to carry around free advertising for them. I don't blame you for it neither."

Fullerton simpered as Scotty examined the checkbook. He seemed to be in two minds.

"Crocodile skin you say?"

"Absolutely. Nothing but the best for our premium clients."

Scotty lodged the pen in his top pocket.

"Now," Fullerton said as he sat down. "Just how much will you be depositing with us?"

Scotty fished a crumpled bill out of his pants pocket. "Try that for a start."

Fullerton flattened out the bill and seemed somewhat crestfallen, mystified even. "Mr. Scott ... One dollar? I ... don't understand."

"What is there not to understand? It's legal money, ain't it?"

Well, yes ... but ... I'd imagined ... You see when you made the appointment to come here I thought you had a substantial deposit in mind."

"Who says I don't?"

"But ..."

"But what? I'll just see how you get along with one dollar first. See, if news was to leak out about how much I keep in here I'd be mighty unhappy. One dollar ought to test the water real good."

"Mr. Scott, I assure you, the details of your bank account will be kept strictly confidential."

"And I believe you, Mr. Fullerton. Really I do." He produced a heartfelt sigh. "You know, my daddy had some mighty sad dealings with banks. That kind of thing sticks in a man's throat. It gives him misconceptions that are hard to shake off."

Fullerton blinked. "I'd be glad to answer any questions you may have about the banking system, Mr. Scott."

"I couldn't help but get the notion that some banks are only really after such folks as are stupid enough to take out a loan and honest enough to pay it back."

"Mr. Scott, let me assure you, we are extremely eager to handle your banking requirements.

"Why's that? Do I look honest and stupid to you?"

"Mr. Scott ... No ... no, not at all."

"Good. Now, listen: have you got any uncut sheets on the premises?"

"Uncut sheets? You mean bills?"

"Yeah. They come in that way from the Treasury, don't they?"

"They do." Fullerton blinked again. The meeting was not going the way he had imagined.

"And as soon as you countersign each bill it becomes legal tender, right?"

"That's correct."

"How many bills are there per sheet?"

"Uh. Twenty-five."

Scotty reached in his pocket and peeled off two $1,000 bills.

"In that case, gimme four signed sheets of 20s. I'll take them as they come. But uncut."

"Uncut?"

"That's what I said. It's legal, ain't it?"

"Well ... yes."

Fullerton rang for the sheets and a teller brought them in. Once the bills were all signed, Scotty rolled them up, wrapped them in a sheet of blotting paper and walked out with them under his arm.

"Thank you, Mr. Fullerton. That's all I want from you for the moment. A pleasure doing business with you."

"Likewise, Mr. Scott," Fullerton said, not quite as sure of himself as he had been fifteen minutes before. "... likewise."

A small, chattering crowd had gathered outside. Scotty waved to them, called back over his shoulder, "I'll be seeing you. You take good care of that money of mine, you hear?"

Scotty turned to the waiting crowd and made sure the reporters had their pencils poised. "A fine bank. Yes, folks! I can definitely say that I am satisfied with the way First Pacific Bank treats their customers."

"Is it true this is the biggest single deposit ever made in a California Bank?" a reporter asked.

"I don't know. What were the others?"

"How much was your deposit, Mr. Scott?" asked another.

"Can't tell you that, boys. It's what they call an undisclosed amount. Now, if you'll just let me go, I have a little business I need to attend to."

An hour later, Warner cornered him in the telegraph office and showed him the front page of the *Examiner*. The headline made interesting reading:

DEATH VALLEY SCOTTY FINDS SMALL CHANGE
TO DINE AT THE BILTMORE.

SCOTT BORROWS $1,000 FROM FELLOW MILLIONAIRE
TO COVER RESTAURANT CHECK.

Warner was not happy, in fact he might easily have been mistaken for a man living in fear of his life. "Didn't I tell you not to be so loud about your money? Garrett must have sent spies to town by now!"

"Yak, yak, yak, yak, yak ... Warner, you're worse than an old washerwoman."

Warner's light frame was brushed aside as Scotty carefully addressed the window clerk: "It's to Albert M. Johnson, 21115 Devonshire Boulevard, North Shore, Chicago, Illinois. Message reads:

LOTS OF DELAYS STOP THERE IS AT LEAST
5 MILLION IN ORE STOP WILL SEND A SACK
JUST AS SOON AS I CAN STOP NEED $1500 TO
GET EIGHT MULE TEAM STOP WIRE IT TO
KEELER STOP DONT SEND NO SHORT MONEY
FOR IT WILL DO ME NO GOOD STOP

As Scotty prepared to leave, he noticed the telegraph clerk's eyes slide across to a no-good ringtail picking his teeth by the door. When the clerk nodded the ringtail nodded back. And when Scotty and his brother went out the door, the ringtail waited a spell, then began to follow.

CHAPTER TEN

Death Valley

SCOTTY TOOK A careful look back though the brightness. Hereabouts the full furnace heat of the day baked the desert salt, dried and cracked the land into astonishing patterns. Here, deep in the Valley, it hadn't rained here in two years.

It was hard for a man to be watchful without looking like he was watching, and that would make him look shifty. Scotty considered the hidden observer who might, at this very moment, be training a telescope on him. To that man, Scotty had no wish to look like anything other than an honest man going about honest work. Still, there was no harm in running an occasional eye along the shimmering horizon, and up along that ridge.

Again, he failed to see anything, but that didn't mean there was nobody up there ...

He knew what was making him think dark thoughts. He was driving his mules right by the place where he found Jeremiah Wilson's body. He saw the grave he had dug and the same old wagon, untouched, except now the horses had been reduced to bleached bones. Scotty walked around it. Windy's tail was down and he looked real hang-dog. She started making the keening noises that border collies make when they feel a loss.

"Hey, now, Windy." He tickled the dog under her chin and she put her ears down and took comfort. "Like I told you before, in this world it's easy come, easy go. There ain't no pockets in a pine board overcoat."

They pressed on and pretty soon Scotty found what he had come for: a stick with a rag on it. He dug out the gravel until he found the top of the buried can, then he unscrewed the cap and inserted a long metal dipper of his own design. It was narrow enough to go in the hole and had enough handle to reach the bottom. He drew out a measure of pure, clear water, drank, wiped his face, fed some water to Windy, then set about pouring water for the mules.

When he'd done, Scotty took out the little blue notebook – the one that had belonged to Wilson. Its dry pages riffled emptily in the wind. There was no clue there. When he had done with the book he put it back in his breast pocket and his eyes happened to catch movement up on the ridge: two distant figures coming over the sky-line. They were on horseback.

Scotty's jaw set grimly. "Windy! Come on. I think we'd best be moving along."

They reached Camp Holdout around sunset. Scotty was clean shaven and washed and waiting. When the two ringtails who had been tailing him broke in on him, they loomed out of the dark like a bad smell. Both were filthy and wore a five day growth of beard. The first ringtail was the mean tooth-picking dude who had followed Scotty out of the telegraph office, except that now he was red-eyed and blistered. He was accompanied by a confederate, a bigger but more twitchy man with staring eyes. They were both in very bad shape.

"We want water!" Ringtail number one croaked.

Scotty, very quiet and calm, feet up and relaxed, with a tin drinking mug in his hand, said, "So you finally got here? You sure took your time getting over the last 40 miles."

"We lost our horses," ringtail number two whispered.

Scotty shook his head "You mean you let them walk off!"

"They broke free!"

"Well, of course they broke free. What do you expect them to do? They were thirsty! They went looking for this." He poured half the water from his mug onto the ground and fixed them with a disgusted stare. "You see what happens when you mistreat animals? This ain't horse country. You bring mules down here, not horses – if you've got any brains at all."

Ringtail number one was angry now, provoked no doubt by the sight of twenty water barrels in back of the cave, or maybe the damp patch in the dust at his feet. He snatched up Scotty's Mauser rifle and pointed it at the owner.

"I told you – we want water!"

Scotty looked back, unperturbed. "I wouldn't deprive a dog of water. But you two'll have to pay for it."

Ringtail number one's reply was half crazed and deadly serious. "Pay for it? Give me some water, or I'll shoot you, you sonofabitch!"

"I said I'd give you water, didn't I? But first you have to put down my rifle. I already took the shells out of it, by the way."

Ringtail number one was actually crying with distress as he threw down the Mauser and drew his own revolver.

"Don't do it, Clarke!" Ringtail number two said. "He's no use dead!"

"To Hell with you!"

"Your pal's right, Clarke," Scotty said. "Dead would be a waste."

But Clarke seemed more comfortable now he was brandishing his revolver. Still shivering from exposure and tortured by thirst, so maybe 'comfortable' would not be the best description.

"Shut up, or I'll put a bullet through your knees right now!"

"No, Clarke, you won't do that either," Scotty said. "Because then you'd be dead too.

"Huh?"

"I got you surrounded, see."

Ringtail number two looked nervously around and peered into the night. He saw nothing.

"Sure you do." Clarke croaked, "All by yourself."

"Ah, but I ain't by myself."

He stood up suddenly and Clarke flinched as if he wasn't the one who was armed to the teeth.

"What you doing?"

"Saving your worthless life." Scotty slowly raised his fingers to his lips and blasted out a three-tone whistle like a bo'sun's pipe. Scotty watched the bad guys quivering. All three were stand there, lit by the fire and surrounded by the dark. They heard the sound of something rustling out there in the desert thirty or forty yards away. The ringtails heard it with surprise and fear.

Scotty shouted. "All right, Bob! That's close enough! Draw your bead on the little guy!"

He whistled again – a different signal this time. The menacing rustle stopped immediately.

"Bob's an Indian friend of mine. He helps with the housework around here. Like he makes sure unexpected guests don't take advantage of the hospitality. And he's just dandy with his pop-gun."

Clarke backed down. As soon as he dropped his hand gun he lost his aggressive attitude too. In fact, he started to beg.

"Please! We've got to have water. Last we had ran out yesterday."

"Oh, there's plenty of water out here. If you know where to look for it."

"Please, let us drink!"

Scotty sighed. "I told you, you can drink. But first, I want to know who sent you."

Ringtail number two began to gush like a west Texas oil well. "A feller back East. Name of Garrett. He said to find your Peerless Mine."

"Did he say anything else?"

"He said once we found it to bury you in it."

Scotty watched them for a while. "Mighty thirsty work you took on there, boys."

He picked up his Peacemaker from the top of a water barrel, twirled it in a fancy way this way and that around his finger, then rapidly put six precisely placed slugs into a kerosene can. And water glugged from the holes.

"Now I don't want to see you boys around here no more. You got that?"

The ringtails were shaken. They nodded furiously.

"All right now, get down and drink your fill."

They got down on their knees and drank gratefully from cupped hands at the water that arched from the holes in the can. They kept it up, without any dignity at all, until the water stopped flowing.

"There's five gallons in that other can," Scotty said. "Enough to get you back the way you come so long as one of you don't steal from the other. Now, let me see you show some willing."

"You're not sending us out there now!" Clarke said.

The other man revealed his secret terror. "There's ... *snakes* at night. What if we should step on one?

Scotty inclined his head. "Should I confiscate your boots so's you don't hurt none of 'em?"

This remark caused the two would-be bushwhackers to halt their negotiating and sling the can on a pole so they could shoulder it as soon as possible and stagger away into the night. It was, they realized simultaneously, probably the best deal they were going to get.

When they'd gone, Scotty waited a little while then let out another modulated whistle. Immediately, the menacing rustle started up again, growing louder until Windy appeared, dragging a rope from her collar. Attached to it was Scotty's coat and a variety of kitchen implements.

Scotty patted his friend. "Windy," he said. "Anybody ever tell you? For a sheep dog, you're a real good wolfhound."

CHAPTER ELEVEN

Chicago, The Johnson Mansion Library

JOHNSON WAS IN his chair with Garrett facing him. He was none too pleased.

"You sent two men out to kill him?"

Garrett folded his arms across his chest. "I sent two men out there to find out if there was a gold mine or not."

"And if there wasn't?"

"Just keeping a tight rein on my investments." Garratt sulked. "Anyway, what's any of this got to do with you?"

"Plenty," Johnson said. "I grubstaked Scott too."

Garrett slapped the leather-bound arms of his seat. "You did *whaaat*?"

"I grubstaked him. Fifty-fifty. Just like you did."

Garrett threw his head back, but instead of seeing a dozen angels as usual, he saw only a half-repaired, half boarded-up vault. "You're crazy! The man's a liar and a fraud!"

"Maybe." Johnson followed Garratt's gaze. "But you should have seen us talking. It was just like we were old friends. I can't put my finger on it, but there's something about that man you just can't help but like. I guess they call it charisma."

"What happened to the angels?" Garrett asked.

"They got shot at."

"Was it Scott who did it?"

"You guessed it."

"So, let me get this right: when he shot up your library you were so impressed with his sunny nature that you threw ten thousand dollars after him?"

Johnson chuckled. "Oh, you know what I'm talking about. A man doesn't get to stay a millionaire unless he's got a –" He searched for the right word. "– an *instinct* about people. From the moment I met that man I knew I just had to go along with him."

Garrett sucked on a back tooth. "Yes, it's called being conned."

Johnson saw that the right moment had arrived. "Well, if you believe he's a confidence trickster then you won't mind if I buy out your share."

Garrett scowled. "Am I hearing you right, Albert?"

"I'll give you what you paid. What would be your problem with that?"

Garrett stared back for a prolonged moment, calculating, then he said, "Oh, no. No, you don't. No, no, no – What have you found out?"

Johnson's shrug was saintly, the shrug of absolute innocence. "Found out? What do you mean?"

"You know exactly what I mean. Come on, Albert. You must think I'm fresh out of the egg!"

"Like I say, I just have this feeling about the man."

"Sure you do."

Johnson decided to switch away from a track that looked like it was about to become a dead end. "Well, Jimmy, if you won't sell your stake to me – then we both have something of a problem."

"And why is that?"

"Because there isn't going to be any gold for either of us."

"How do you work that out?"

"Well, you see, it's all a question of incentive. It's like this – you own 50%, and I own 50%. And that means Scotty owns ..."

Johnson shrugged again.

Garrett saw the problem. "Nothing?" he said.

"That's right. The kind of nothing that's worth exactly one hundred take away twice fifty."

Garrett began to nod hollowly. "Why should he go out there and dig when he has to turn everything he finds over to you and me? Albert, this is your fault."

"Let's not get into pointing blame," Johnson said evenly. "The question is: what are we going to do about it? The important thing is that we induce him to sign a new contract." He opened a drawer and took out a document. "This way, each of the three of us will take a third."

Garrett looked the paper over with disgust. "You're asking me to give away 17% of my ownership? To that ... *bushwhacker*?"

"It's exactly the same loss I'm prepared to take."

Garrett pushed the contract away. "I won't do it!"

Johnson pushed it back. "Listen, Jimmy: a third of something is a whole lot better than a half of nothing. Isn't that right?"

As Garrett struggled with the inescapable end-point of Johnson's logic, the latter's solemn-faced butler came in with a telegram served on a silver tray and garnished with an ivory letter opener. Johnson tore open the envelope and pulled out the flimsy paper. He read silently:

NEED NEW SADDLES STOP SEND $500 SOONEST STOP

Johnson looked up indulgently. "Now, come on, Jimmy. What do you say? Give an old friend a break here."

CHAPTER TWELVE

Los Angeles, California

IT WAS LATE afternoon and Scotty was walking happily along the sidewalk. In the road, automobiles were spluttering by, frightening the horses. Construction was everywhere. Big buildings were shooting up, ten or a dozen floors some of them. There were stables and printers and grocery businesses, linen laundries and dairies and lumber stores along every road. Things were changing so fast it was hard for a man to keep track of exactly where he was.

Scotty came to the street corner where the Italian florist stood.

"Hey, Tony! You did what we talked about?"

Tony gave him a professional smile. "All set up for you, Mr. Scott. All waiting beautiful in the Mermaid Bar."

Scotty pulled out his legendary bankroll and started peeling. Outside people had begun to gather. One or two were even bold enough to come in. Scotty knew they were watching him rather than interesting themselves in the floral displays. Every bill he peeled off was a hundred. He somehow found a lowly ten and looked at it in disgust, ripped it into pieces and threw it down. He offered a hundred."

Tony was apologetic. "Scotty ... you know I can't change that."

"So take it to a bank."

"They ain't open."

"Banks! Always happy to take money off of you, but not near so anxious to pay it out again. Did I tell you, they got a dollar of mine in one?"

"Yeah, I bet!"

"It's the God's honest truth."

Scotty tore the hundred dollar bill in two, tucked one half in his pocket and gave the other half to Tony. "Take fifty on account. Get my change for tomorrow. I'm going over to the Mermaid Bar right now to see what you done for me."

There was a posse of maybe fifty people following him as he walked to his favorite hotel. When he walked, they walked. When he stopped, they stopped. None of them dared come up close to him, they just wanted to trail after a man who'd had so many words written about him in the newspapers.

As he entered the hotel lobby, Lars the Swede came up to him. He was flustered, "Scotty, don't you go in dat bar."

"Lars, I told Kate I'd see her, here. I got a surprise lined up and everything."

"I know, dat. But we got a bunch of no goods come in. I think they looking for trouble. Maybe wid you. Your gold mine's all they been talking about."

"So throw 'em out."

"There's four of 'em!"

"Call the cops."

"What for? They didn't do nothing wrong yet. And their money is yoost as good as anybody else's."

Scotty waved Lars' objections aside, but as he entered the Mermaid Bar someone he'd never seen before asked him: "Hey, gold miner. You need a drink?" And there was laughter at somebody's expense.

Scotty appraised the man in a flash: he was a *weasel*. "Drink? Sure I need drink. A man gets a powerful thirst on him out in Death Valley."

"And when was the last time you was out there?"

"That's for me to know." Scotty looked around, saw several familiar faces – the usual crew, but they were hanging back in an unusual fashion. He grinned at the weasel. "But I'll tell you what: I bet I can drink booze quicker than anybody else in this place."

Next to the weasel was a big guy, and behind him two others who seemed to lack social sophistication.

"Oh, yeah?" the big man said.

"Yeah," Scotty affirmed amiably. "Scott's the name. Everyone calls me Death Valley Scotty."

"Yeah, we heard of you."

"Well, that's no surprise. Most folks have."

"I read about you in the paper. And they said the reason you drink so good is you got a real big mouth."

The usual faces who were hanging back, hung even further back. The big guy snickered to his two pals, who snickered back. Neither specimen exactly came across as a college professor, but if they had been, then the big guy would have been their dean.

"Nope, the reason I drink is because I like the taste."

"I bet you think you're pretty smart, don't you cowboy?"

"All right, genius," Scotty said. "Since you're a betting man, how about my hundred against your ten that you can't beat me in a drinking contest with rules?"

"I'll go for that."

"Oh, gooooood." Scotty smiled, then turned to the barman. "Sam, gimme a glass of beer, a two quart jug and a shot of Jack. Alrighty, here's the rules. First I'm gonna drink down a pint of beer just to whet my whistle and you're gonna watch me do it. In case you get any smart ideas, you can't touch my beer glass or my jug, and I can't touch your shot. With me so far?"

The big guy nodded, none too certain. "I got that."

"Now soon as my beer glass hits the deck, then I'm gonna start in on that two quart jug. You're gonna count to three to give me a head start and then you're gonna reach for the Jack. Now, I bet you a hundred dollars to your ten that I can drink off my two quarts before you can down that shot."

While the professors looked to their dean, the big guy said, "You got yourself a touch of the sun, Mister."

"Think so? Then show me the color of your money."

The big guy got his pals to search their pockets and together they mustered up ten bucks in change.

Scotty braced himself. "Ready? – By the way, counting goes 'One, Two, Three', all right? Here we go."

He took a theatrically deep breath then chugged down the pint of beer in six seconds flat. Fast drinking, but not the Tonsil Town Open Throat record by any means. As the empty glass hit the deck the big guy started his count.

"One, two ..."

Scotty started to reach for the jug, but then neatly picked up his empty beer glass turned it over and slammed it down over the shot glass. Then he leaned back and started drinking in a leisurely way from the jug.

The big guy looked like he'd been shot. "Hey!"

Scotty raised a finger at him. "A – a – ah! You can't touch my glass!"

Sam the barman laughed, then stopped. The big guy and his pals didn't think much of the trick, and when Scotty scooped the armful of change into his Stetson. The big guy said, "You cheated!"

Scotty stepped to the window and threw the coins out into the street.

"Come on, boys and girls. Candy money time!"

Then he stepped back to the bar.

"You saying I cheated now?" He tucked a hundred dollar bill into the big guy's shirt pocket. "That's for you. Now you can't say I don't have a sense of humor."

The big guy was perplexed for a moment. He fished out the hundred and stared at it.

"It's O.K. It's good." Scotty told him. "Go take a drink on me. Buy your pals one too. It's only money."

The big guy produced a big cheesy grin. "Know what? You're not such a bad feller after all."

"I know it." Scotty turned to the rest of his pals, the usual ones who had been hanging back. "Hey, hey. I got a great one for you. Give me ten dollars, somebody."

One of the bar crowd gave him a ten.

"What's this, Teddy, your week's pay?"

"The best part of it," Teddy admitted.

"And they say trust is dead. All righty – watch close now. It's called 'Money to Burn'.

Scotty got into his showman's stance and with a flourish he carefully rolled the bill up lengthwise like a cigar, struck a match off his boot heel and lit it up. The paper tube just set fire and burned down. Everyone gawked at it happening and when the flame reached the end, Scotty stubbed it into an ashtray, and clapped the dust off his hands. Everyone was still looking at him expectantly.

"There, now. Wasn't that fun?"

Teddy looked at him uncomprehendingly. "Well, where's the trick in that?"

"Ain't no trick. Did I say it was a trick?"

Teddy scrabbled in the ashtray for the burned out stub.

Everyone laughed – except Teddy.

"That was my ten!"

"What's the matter, got a sentimental attachment to it?"

Scotty peeled off a bill from his bankroll. "Here, dry your eyes on one of these. Look close, you'll see double zero – just like the kerosene."

"Hey! That's a hundred!"

"Sam'll break it for you. The drinks are on me tonight, everybody."

There was an instant scramble towards the bar. Scotty turned away from the circle of fun as he noted Gaylord approaching.

"Hey, Zee. You just missed all the fun."

"So I see." Gaylord tilted his head in a notably self-satisfied way. "Truth is I been having a little fun of my own today."

Scotty raised his eyebrows. "Well, if you don't look like the cat that got the cream."

"Remember I told you about my friend at the Santa Fe Railroad?"

"Yup."

"Well, he just told me that Santa Fe's bidding on the U.S. Mail contract."

"Mail? Is there money in that?"

Gaylord looked smug. "Are you kidding me? It's foolproof money. Gold mines run out of gold, and the press are fickle – one minute they're building you up, next minute they're tearing you down again. But people will always need to write to one another. That's something you can depend on."

Scotty nodded accepting the point, but not wanting to admit that he wasn't big on writing letters when a telegram would get there quicker.

"And if things go according to plan," Gaylord said. "I'll soon be handling the Santa Fe end of the U.S. Mail negotiation."

Scotty dwelt on that for a second or two. "You know, Zee, what the Santa Fe needs is a real big whoop-de-doodle."

"Come again."

"You know what a whoop-de-doodle is. Something shiny and loud to catch the attention of the folks they're trying to impress. A whoop-de-doodle Buffalo Bill style!"

Frank Sanders came in with a I-just-had-a-bitch-of-a-day face on him. He took a whiskey off the bar and slammed it, sitting all the while on the tail of Scotty's words.

"That Buffalo Bill stuff is dead and buried," he growled. "This is a new century in case you haven't noticed, cowpuncher."

"I seen it coming, all right," Scotty said.

"It don't look like it to me. These days people are more interested in automobiles and moving pictures than horses and six-shooters."

Scotty snorted. "Aw, people don't change. Everyone always liked a good show."

Sanders let out a sour breath. He was like a horse in harness that knew it had two more hours of hard pulling to go and didn't much care for it. "You mean like throwing other people's money around? After a while that kind of thing gets to be a helluva yawn."

Scotty weighed the unexplained change in Sanders' attitude. "What's the matter, Frank? Somebody scoop your ice cream?"

When Sanders said nothing by way of reply, Gaylord caught Scotty's eye with a significant look. It translated as: "What-was-I-just-telling-you?" And when Sanders moved away, Scotty asked, "What do you suppose is eating old Frank?"

Gaylord said, "My guess is that William Randolph God-Almighty has been swatting at his butt to come up with something else new and sensational. It's no easy thing to be a newspaper man day-in-day-out."

Scotty nodded. "Well, then, we've gotta help him out, don't we?"

But before Gaylord could rise to that remark, Kate came in and Scotty kissed her and showed her the huge spray of roses up against the far wall. The red buds spelled out her name.

"Oh, Scotty? Are they for me?" she said with enthusiasm.

Scotty shouted round the bar. "Anybody else called 'Kate' in here?"

Kate's embarrassment go the better of her. "Scotty ... please!"

"Now, do you believe I love you?" Turning to Gaylord and Sanders he said, "Never did meet a woman that didn't need that said a hundred times a day. We're dining at the Biltmore tonight, fellers."

As Kate dutifully inspected the flowers, Gaylord made a swift aside to Scotty. "Come on, give the gal a break. Can't you see you're embarrassing her? You're powerful company for a stay at home gal like that."

"Stay at home, nothing! I take her everywhere. Show me the

woman who don't like to be made a fuss out of, and I'll show you a man."

Scotty snapped his fingers to a figure near the door, then he took Kate by the arm and turned her to face a photographer who came in with a big black bellows camera on a tripod that was almost as tall as he was.

"Come on, Kate," he told her. "Smile for the picture."

She smiled, but he saw that it was not a smile of genuine pleasure.

"So long fellers! We're off to eat."

There was a chorus of goodbyes as Scotty led Kate out of the Mermaid Bar, through the lobby and into the back of a driven car.

"Do we really have to eat at the Biltmore?" Kate asked as they settled.

"Can't think of nowhere better. Can you?"

"Can't we just go to a regular place?"

A regular place? What do you want with a regular place?"

"I'd just rather we did."

Scotty thought about that, saw that she was serious and told the driver, "Take us to Lannigan's."

"No. Not even Lannigan's."

Scotty felt her stiffen. "What then?"

She pointed out the window to a modestly-priced place they happened to be passing.

"That would suit me fine."

Scotty's brows knitted, though he tried not to show his disappointment. "Anything you want."

At Kate's prompting, they took a table for two in the corner – the darkest corner.

"It don't look so bad in here, he said, taking her hand across the table. He smiled at her. "Kate, I think you got real good taste."

"You do?"

"You're out with me, ain't ya?"

She didn't rise to his joke, but kept on with her serious face. "Am I out with you, Scotty? We never seem to have any time alone."

Scotty scratched the back of his neck, then said defensively. "Don't I take you out to lots of places? Don't we visit all the high spots together? Don't I always show you a good time?"

"Of course you do. But what I meant was *ordinary* time. Just you and me and no ... no showmanship."

Scotty stared back at her like she had just asked him to name the capital of Venezuela.

She tried harder. "You know, a man and a woman need to get to know one another."

Scotty pointed his thumbs at his chest. "Well ... here I am. What else do you want to know about me?"

She smiled at him, touched by his lack of understanding. "You know, when we're together I can't help thinking about how long it'll be before you have to go back out into the desert again."

"Maybe that'll change. To listen to Zee talk, you'd think there was more gold to be had in town than out in the desert.

She let a second or two pass, then said. "I don't like that man. I didn't from the moment I set eyes on him.

"Oh, Zee's all right. I don't know what's gotten into Frank Sanders though.

"You're pretty friendly with all those newspaper people aren't you?

"It's them that's friendly with me." He looked down at the table. "Or it used to be."

"Is that how our picture got into the papers last time we had dinner together? And that story about how Millionaire Bill loaned you all that money."

Scotty spread his hands. "I can't help it if newspaper reporters wait in ambush on me wherever I go. I'm what you call a regular celebrity. Ain't nothing much to be done about it."

Kate was unimpressed. "But you invited them, didn't you?

"There's bound be two or three of them around all the time.

Kate put her hand over his. "That wasn't dinner for two we had. It was a publicity stunt."

As if coming to the rescue a brass blonde waitress sidled up. Between words she was chewing on a wad of something in one side of her mouth. Her breasts were, Scotty decided, something worthy of note.

"So. How ya doing, Cowboy?"

"I'm doing just fine."

"How's about a little red hot chili tonight?" She sort wriggled as she asked.

"Oh, I'll take me some of that. And -?"

"Chicken please," Kate said coolly

Scotty smiled broadly at the waitress. "And breast of chicken for the lady."

"Lady, huh?" The waitress darted a dagger glance at Kate, then opened up another sugary smile for Scotty. "So. Like what ya see – on the menu?"

Kate's eyes narrowed. "Why, you floozy!

The waitress masticated her gum for a moment. "Who's your friend, gold miner? Clementine? Or just Plain Jane?"

She turned on her heel and walked off too fast for Kate to think up a sufficiently cutting reply. To Scotty she said, "What was she chewing on? The cud?"

"Oh, that. It's a newfangled thing. They call it 'gum'."

"Well, it looks a long way from classy. And so does she."

Scotty shook his head. "Now you know why I wanted to take you to someplace a little more up market. At least there the folks who recognize a person are good enough to behave as if they don't."

Kate was suddenly serious again. "Scotty, are you for real? Please tell me you are."

"You keep asking me that same question, and I keep giving you the same answer. I'm for real. It's just that I don't seem that way to some people sometimes."

The waitress returned, put down two big plates in front of them. "Here, cowboy. Why don't I tuck in your napkin for you?"

As she leaned forward there came the heavy scent of gardenias. Scotty felt as if he was staring into the Grand Canyon. "That waitressing uniform sure don't leave a whole lot to the imagination, does it?"

The waitress returned an appreciative smile. "Imagine all you want."

As she took to waitressing elsewhere Scotty shook his head. It was like he was breaking a spell. Kate was still fuming.

"I saw the way you were looking at her," she said unnecessarily. "I sometimes think you'd be better off with a girl like that."

"Naw! I had her marked the moment she came up, all sidewinding like that. What do you think?"

"Shame on you. You were encouraging her."

"I wouldn't even let my dog bark at her."

"Oh, Scotty," she said, earnest all of a sudden. "I wish you weren't going back out into the desert again."

Scotty let that pass. It was always best with outbursts, the more earnest they were, the more you had to avoid them.

"It ain't just gold, you know," he said after a space of silence.

"No?"

"You know what I think? I think everybody ought to have to have a secret place. A place that only that person knows about."

Kate looked strangely at him. "I never did have a place like that. I never knew I needed one."

"Well, I think everybody needs one. A place you can go to think, be at peace with yourself, a place where you can listen to the quiet and let it heal your soul."

She looked into his eyes, captivated by his sudden turn of romanticism. "And your place is in Death Valley?

"My place is in Death Valley." He stirred from his reverie. "Come on. If the waitress in here is getting to you, let's go someplace else. We'll go for a walk. Just you and me. Los Angeles is a good place to walk alone at night."

They got ready to leave, then Scotty called to the waitress. "We changed our minds. Don't worry I'll pay for what we ordered."

"Great! Just when I get the man who gives out the good tips."

"Sure. And I got a good tip for you."

"You do?

"Yeah, I do." He took her by the upper arm and turned her away from Kate, at the same time tucking ten dollars into her cleavage. "It's the best tip I ever got," he said, making sure Kate heard. "Never play leapfrog with a unicorn."

CHAPTER THIRTEEN

Los Angeles, Santa Fe Station

A PIERCING TRAIN whistle and blasts of steam heralded Scotty's arrival on the platform. He was carrying a big leather bag. On top, sitting between the handles, was what looked like a two foot-long roll of blotting paper tied up with string.

He wandered along the platform looking for the ideal spot, then boarded the train car and eventually sat down at a window, looking both ways up and down the track like a man plotting mischief.

Finally satisfied, he put his bag on the seat beside him, then put his feet up, tilted his hat forward over his eyes and folded his arms as if attempting to manage forty winks.

Next thing he knew he woke up to find the train slowing down. It was arriving at a station, and he didn't have long to wait to find out which one because the conductor was coming through Scotty's car. He was a man of about fifty, with a beaky face, gray mustache and eyes like oysters.

"San Bernardino!" the man called out, and ten paces later he yelled, "San Bernardino, California!" as if his customers usually didn't know where they were.

Scotty remained motionless as the conductor passed. He settled back down and the next thing he knew the train was slowing again. This time the conductor was already moving around Scotty's car.

"Barstow!" the conductor said, and ten paces later. "Barstow, California!"

Scotty got up as the conductor passed and prepared to leave the car. He took his bag with him. The blotting paper roll was still there on top of it, so without further delay he got down from the train.

He chose a bench seat on a shady part of the platform under a big station sign that read "BARSTOW". He sat down and waited. In the meantime he took out a General Arthur cigar and lit it. Nearby was a poster that made startling claims:

Every discriminating smoker has experiencedthe annoyance of being obliged to put up with inferior cigars while traveling. You can avoidthis always and be sure of a reliable and

Porto Rico, he thought. Well, there's a thing. And he checked his watch for the first time.

Pretty soon after he'd checked his watch for the fourth time, coming in the opposite direction was another train. It made a lot of noise as it pulled in. Scotty got up and readied himself to leave, enjoying the emphatic clanging and rushing of steam and squealing of brakes.

A few people got down, a few others boarded. Then Tom Ripley, a grizzled railroad official who Scotty vaguely knew approached. "Mr. Scott, didn't I see you just get off a train from Los Angeles about an hour back?"

"Yup."

"All you did was just sit there. And now you're going right back?"

"I only come for the fishing," Scotty told him, "but it looks like the tide's out."

Ripley glanced at him like he was nuts and went about his business.

"Passengers for San Bernardino and Los Angeles. All Aboard!"

Scotty climbed into a Pullman car and carefully chose a place to sit. He put his big leather bag on the seat beside him and checked that his two foot-long roll of blotting paper was still secure. Then he put his feet up, tilted his hat forward over his eyes and folded his arms as if going to sleep.

This time, he stayed awake. Across the aisle were two gentlemen, at least they could be taken for gentlemen because they were dressed in Eastern business clothes. Scotty had a feeling that since they were disguised as upright citizens, they might be just the sort of men he was looking for.

That feeling only grew.

One of them gave him a snooty look when he put his boots up on the opposite seat, but then his eyes slid to Scotty's bag and the paper roll on top. Some men, it seemed, judged other men by the quality of their luggage.

Outside, the Mojave desert rolled by. Scotty roused himself, as if from a particularly rewarding nap. He pushed back his hat and stretched luxuriously.

"Yaaaaaaaaaaaahh! Hoooo!"

He shook his head, laced his fingers and cracked his knuckles, then turned to the two gentlemen across the aisle.

"Nothing like forty winks on a train, eh, fellers?"

"One turned away. The other nodded in a reserved, I-don't-want-to-get-involved-with-you sort of way. This, though they did not know it, was like waving a red rag at a rodeo.

Fortunately, just then, a Pullman attendant came by. "Hey, Charlie!" Scotty yelled at him. "Over here!"

The Attendant came, looked expectant. "Can I help you, sir?"

"You sure can. You got any of that Cham-pag-nee?"

"Cham-pag-nee, sir?"

"That's what it looked like when I saw it wrote on a label. Fancy new drink from Paris, France."

"Uh, you mean 'champagne', sir?"

Scotty nodded, "Shampayne, yeah, that's probably the stuff. I'll have a bottle of that. And a couple of whisky chasers." He turned to the two gentlemen. "Any of you two fellers want a drink?"

The first gentleman demurred, his time with excessive politeness. "No, thank you."

Scotty recoiled in a good natured way from that. "Oh, c'mon! It an opportunity. All the drinks are on me today. What do you say?"

By now the first gentleman was pretty certain he didn't want to get drawn in. "Really, no."

Scotty took the point like a man at ease. "You fellers Mormons?" He turned to the waiting attendant. "Bring over three glasses with that bottle anyhow. These fellers don't know they're thirsty yet."

The attendant seemed glad to depart.

Scotty grinned. "So. Where you boys from?"

Gentleman number one put on one of those patient expressions usually reserved for the irritating pan-handler. "Chicago."

Scotty was impressed. "Chicago, huh? I heard of that. They say it's a pretty big place." He seemed to let it drop, then said, "So, you in the meat packing business?"

"Ah, no."

Scotty nodded again, thoughtfully. "Uh-huh. Well, now, there's a coincidence. Cuz I ain't neither."

Just then – fortunately – the attendant returned with the drinks.

"Sir, that'll be twelve dollars and thirty-five cents."

Scotty smiled back. "Just a minute."

He went into his bag, drew out a large pair of scissors, snipped off the ties that held his roll together and opened it out. There, revealed, were his uncut sheets of $20 bills. He carefully snipped out the bill from the corner of the first sheet and handed it to the attendant, whose eyes were round at the method of payment.

"S'all right. It's good. And you can keep the change."

The attendant examined the bill. He seemed more than a little hesitant, but the prospect of profiting to the tune of seven dollars and sixty-five cents, which was a sizeable portion of his weekly wage, had doubtless set him thinking. Eventually, he said, "Thank you, sir."

When the attendant had gone, gentleman number two began to take more than a passing interest. "Say – mind if I take a look at that?"

Scotty beamed at him. "Why, sure!"

Scotty snipped off another bill and passed it across. Then he snipped off a third and passed it to gentleman number one. The Chicagoans made a big deal out of examining the bills. They felt them, turned them over, looked closely at them, wet them with spit and rubbed at them then examined their finger ends. They sniffed them, compared them to one of their own, and generally scrutinized them like hounds that are onto something.

Scotty watched the entire rigmarole with a smile on his face. "Pretty good, don't you think?"

Gentleman number two said stealthily: "Extraordinarily good." He glanced at his friend, then said, "Where did you ... where did you *get* them?"

Scotty's toothsome smile broadened still further. "Ahhh, no," he said. "Now, that would be telling. But I'm real proud of them."

"I'll bet," gentleman number one said.

Scotty offered his hand. "Folks call me Death Valley Scotty on account of that's where I make my money."

"Is that a fact?" gentleman number two asked.

"Yup. And pretty soon they're gonna be calling me 'Los Angeles Scotty' on account of that's where I'm gonna be spending it."

The two gentlemen exchanged more glances.

Gentleman number one, who had been making all the running so far, said, "How *exactly* do you make your money, ah, Scotty?"

Scotty winked. "It's all right to tell you fellers."

He picked up his leather bag and banged it down on the floor of the car. It clanged with a muffled, heavy cast-metal sound.

The train ate up the miles between Barstow and San Bernardino and, beyond it, a hot but mellow afternoon developed into a layered pastel sunset. The beautiful landscape just kind of *pulled* the train through it along an endless straight.

Now, a steam train plowing across a wilderness is always a sight for sore eyes, and often a joy to those within, but on this occasion at least three of the passengers had their thoughts on something other than the beauty of the American West. And that was just as well.

As the Mojave continued to slide past the window of the Pullman car, Walter Scott talked with the pronounced gestures of a boastful fisherman to two gentlemen, whose demeanors were now ones of rapt attention. The more Scotty drank, the more boastful the fisherman became, until he had landed the equivalent of an 80 pound salmon. What the two gentlemen from back East hardly guessed was that this gigantic fish was merely bait for something even bigger.

Pretty soon the train began slowing down and the conductor, a slimmer man this time with a blond mustache and side whiskers, began his familiar round.

"San Bernardino!" Ten paces, then: "San Bernardino, California!"

Scotty was in the middle of telling a tale about the Old Days. His voice was slurred and there were four champagne bottles stacked up by his elbow.

"So I says to Buffalo Bill ... I says ..."

Gentleman number one got up as the conductor passed and prepared to leave the car.

When he had gone, Gentleman number two waited a moment then interrupted Scotty's tale at a critical juncture. "'Scuse me, won't you? Been on this damned train three days. I gotta stretch my legs."

Undeterred, Scotty called after him, "I says to Buffalo Bill ... 'You ain't nothing but a sonofabitch liar!' And he says to me, 'Scotty, you're right! But at least I know when to keep my goddamn mouth shut!'"

He laughed uproariously since there was no one else nearby to do it for him.

Then he sat back and pushed his hat forward over his eyes, a move that did not stop him from seeing out of the corner of one of them as far as the yellow lights of the San Bernardino telegraph office. It was very simple, Scotty thought, to figure out what was being said and done inside:

Gentleman number two, would be much more sober than he had been thirty seconds before. He would be leaning in on the clerk, and saying, "I want to send an urgent wire."

66

The telegraph clerk would be asking, as they always did: "Where to?"

And gentleman number two would say, "The Los Angeles County Sheriff's Department" – or words to that effect.

Just as soon as gentleman number two came back into the railroad car and settled down, Scotty offered him an apologetic smile.

"'Scuse me. Is this San Bernardino?" he asked, like one bewildered.

"That's what the sign says."

"It does? That's good. Only, I got a little business to attend to – gotta make me a hotel reservation."

He got up a little unsteadily, and got off the train, taking his bag with him.

Once inside the San Bernardino telegraph office Scotty – much more sober than he was thirty seconds before – leaned in on the clerk.

"I want to send an urgent wire," he said.

"Where to?" the telegraph clerk asked, as telegraph clerks couldn't help but do.

"The *Los Angeles Examiner*."

Scotty wrote out the text, paid the clerk and left. The clerk watched him go, then took an incoming message and looked at it with excitement. Then he quickly shut up shop and took the message across the street to the San Bernardino Sheriff's office.

As the train began to pull out of San Bernardino, a tall, dour, flint-eyed lawman by the name of Sheriff John C. Ralphs leapt for the foot board. He was every inch a lawman. He came to Scotty's car, then chose a vacant seat in the corner.

The lawman watched what was going on, which was: Scotty telling stories and two Chicagoans laughing at what he said. This went on all the way to Los Angeles. And when the train began to pull into Santa Fe Station, Ralphs got up, came over to Scotty all but for two paces of distance, drew a revolver and showed his badge.

This action powerfully affected the other passengers, whose shocked reaction was testament to their curiosity and general excitability.

"My name is Sheriff John C. Ralphs," the lawman announced with the kind of formality only lawmen can muster. "Put both your hands where I can see them."

Scotty put them forward as if presenting them for a fingernail inspection.

Ralphs said, "Stand up. Turn around. Put your hands behind you."

Scotty said innocently, "What's this all about, Sheriff Ralphs? Do you have to point that thing at me?"

This is the sort of remark that does not impress any kind of lawman. After all, they are just doing their job.

"Just do as you are told," Ralphs said.

Then he took out a pair of handcuffs, handed them out toward gentleman number two, and said, "I'd be obliged if you'd put them on him."

At first, Scotty was surprised that Ralphs thought him such a danger that he needed to keep him covered from a distance of two paces. But when Scotty thought about it some, he realized that the Sheriff probably had no idea what a harmless and unarmed fellow he was actually dealing with. It was probably a case of there being old lawmen and bold lawmen, but no old, bold lawmen. He decided that Ralphs was right to take no chances.

Gentleman number two was as obliging as any upright citizen could possibly be. "Certainly, Sheriff," he said to Ralphs, then added helpfully: "Those are the bills right there!"

Gentleman number one picked up the sheets and unrolled them for inspection.

Scotty said to Sheriff Ralphs, "Hey! Tell that ringtail to get his paws off of my cash!"

Ralphs rolled his eyes, more confident now that he was in complete control, and said, "Sit down and shut up."

Although it was not an order an average person could mistake for another, still Scotty felt able to protest. "But that's my money! Are you arresting me?"

At this point, gentleman number one said, "And he said he's got the printing plates right there, in his bag."

Scotty opened his mouth wide. "That is a downright lie. I never said nothing of the kind. Sheriff Ralphs, are you arresting me?"

But Ralphs only replied, "You are damned right I'm arresting you."

"What for?" he asked, and when no answer came he tried: "For what?"

"Counterfeiting," Ralphs said. "Now sit down!"

There was a squeal of brakes as the train drew into the terminal. Scotty sat down as the car lurched to a halt. Immediately, a posse of uniformed police and official-looking types came aboard the train. There was a moment of confusion as the other passengers were moved along.

Scotty faced the two Chicagoans. "Is this your doing?" he asked.

"It is," they said with one voice.

"And after all that liquor I bought for you fellers?"

"You better pipe down," Gentleman number one said with marked relish. "You're gonna serve a long sentence for this."

Gentleman number two added. "Yes. You will find this is no small matter."

"Well," Scotty told them, emphasizing his words with abandon. "I ain't *never* seen *such* ingratitude in all my *born* days."

At this, gentleman number two said, poisonously triumphant, "You thought you'd get away with it, didn't you? I shouldn't be surprised if there was a reward in it for us."

"My money is as real as yours, only far quicker in the spending I dare say. And probably a whole lot realer, seeing as I earned it fair and square and not by taking rewards."

Sheriff Ralphs said, "You can tell that to these gentlemen. They're Treasury officials."

Photographers began to jostle at the window with their big bellows cameras and flash pans. Reporters were behind them, shouting questions and other comments.

Scotty told Gentleman number one: "You are a prize ringtail, and no better than you ought to be!" Then he turned to Gentleman number two and said, "And you – you are next to a fool!"

Sheriff Ralphs said, "Hey, you! I told you to shut up, so shut up!"

At which Scotty appealed to heaven, saying "So many free schools, and yet so much ignorance in the land! I declare, I do not know what to make of it."

CHAPTER FOURTEEN

Los Angeles, Central Jail

LOS ANGELES CENTRAL Jail was at at First Street, between Broadway and Hill. Scotty found himself being led inside that august institution from the back of a police wagon and still in handcuffs. Ralphs followed, as did a crowd of witnesses and policemen and half a dozen reporters.

When Ralphs hauled Scotty up in front of the worldly duty sergeant he waited until things had quietened down and then he took off Scotty's handcuffs.

"Name?" the duty sergeant said in an Irish accent.

Before Ralphs could speak Scotty said, "Walter E. Scott – that's three T's."

"What's the charge?"

Ralphs looked narrowly at his captive. "Counterfeiting."

The duty sergeant's eyebrows lifted. He seemed so impressed that Scotty wondered if he now ranked higher or lower in the scheme of things than a common or garden murderer.

"You the arresting officer?"

"I am," Ralphs declared.

The duty sergeant shook his head and mused, "Death Valley Scotty, eh? ... who would have thought this was the way he was making it?"

A Treasury official unrolled one of the sheets on the side table and commenced to go over it minutely with a big magnifying glass.

Scotty pulled away from his handler. "Hey! That's my money he's fooling with!"

"That ain't money," Ralphs told him. "That's evidence!"

The Treasury official looked up. He was mightily uncomfortable. So much so that he might have been wearing tweed underpants.

"It's good," he said unhappily. "Very good. In fact, the best I've ever seen. But it's clearly counterfeit."

"Counterfeit my jack-ass!" Scotty yelled at him with all the righteous indignation he could gather together at such short notice. "You, sir, are nothing but a no-good ringtail!"

70

The duty sergeant sighed an Irish sigh, stuck his pen back in the inkwell and said to one of his uniformed men, "Martin, lock him up!"

Next morning came slowly as they have a habit of doing in jails, but not so slowly as they do to the guilty. Scotty, of course, was innocent. He was lying on the comfortless bunk when he heard footsteps in the corridor. He sat up and saw Kate. With her came a jailer and Z. Beldon Gaylord. The jailer started to unlock the cell.

"Oh, Scotty!" Kate cried the moment she saw him. "Are you all right?

"The bed's a mite hard, and it don't smell too good, but what would you expect from the cheapest hotel in town?"

"Not so cheap," Gaylord said. "I just posted a five hundred dollar bond. And look at this."

He held up a copy of the *Los Angeles Examiner*. The front page headline read:

DEATH VALLEY SCOTTY A COUNTERFEITER

True Source of the Golf Miner's Wealth Revealed

"Frank Sanders has just torn down everything you built up." Gaylord told him. "I never thought I'd see you do this to yourself. I thought you were smarter than that."

The door opened and Kate rushed into his arms.

"Oh, Scotty, this is a nightmare. Tell me it's not happening."

Scotty hugged her, and then took her by the arms and held her away from him so he could look her square in the face.

"Faith!" he told her. "That's what you need at a time like this. Got it?"

She nodded none too certainly. "But Scotty, just look at the shameful things they're saying about you in the newspaper. I thought Frank Sanders was your friend."

"When Humpty-Dumpty climbed up on that big old wall," Scotty said archly, "he should have known what was coming to him."

"Never mind nursery rhymes!" Gaylord threw his hat down on

71

the bunk. "You've really blown it so far as this town is concerned. All deals are off now."

Scotty showed his unconcern. "Ah, what you beefing about? The day I can't handle a bunch of ringtails is the day I leave this town. And as for Frank Sanders being my friend, he's a newspaperman. They don't have any friends – neither before nor after they join the profession."

Gaylord poked a finger at Scotty's breastbone. "I want my five hundred back from you the minute you get out of here!"

"Oh!" Kate told him. "How can you be so mercenary at a time like this?"

"Because, my dear," he told her loftily, "I am a man of *business*."

"Ah, stop your sweating, Zee. This is all a complicated misunderstanding. But it certainly serves to show a man who his true friends are. You'll have your money directly."

"I'll believe that when I see it."

"Then keep at least one eye open and you won't miss it."

Right around this time, the jailer, who had been listening to all the badinage with limited interest decided he had had quite enough.

"Come on," he growled. "Get outa here. It's check out time!"

They came up to the front desk and approached the duty sergeant.

"Hey, I want all my stuff," Scotty told him. "And what's this about Mr. Gaylord here posting five hundred for my bail?"

"That's what it was set at," the duty sergeant said. "That's what he paid."

"Five hundred for being *drunk*?"

"It wasn't being drunk you were locked up for. It was counterfeiting."

Scotty presented himself as the man who could solve the sergeant's biggest problem. "What if I can clear this up right here and now?"

The duty sergeant smiled back indulgently. "And how, pray, are you gonna do that?"

Scotty turned to Kate and said, "I got a job for you. Get over to First Pacific and tell the Bank President he's wanted here urgent. Tell him I sent you."

Kate rushed off.

Scotty turned back to the desk sergeant. "Is that arresting officer still here?"

The Duty sergeant glanced up at the wall clock. "He's at La Grande depot. His train leaves in just under an hour."

"Get him back here, with as many of them Treasury fellers as you like."

The sergeant tilted over his head. "And why should I do that?"

"Because if you don't I'll have Mr. Gaylord here un-post my bail, and that'll mean I'll have to stay in your cells."

"That would be no skin off my nose."

"I could be here for weeks."

"So what?"

"Sergeant, do you really want your precinct to be besieged night and day by photographers and newspaper reporters? It would be like being overrun by giant rats."

"Rats?"

"Giant ones. Think what your lieutenant would say. Think about your evaporating peace of mind. They don't pay a man in your position enough for that kind of tribulation."

The vision had been painted, and it was a vision of chaos and strife, the kind of vision that did not sit well with an orderly mind. The duty sergeant looked into the future and disliked what he saw.

"On the whole," he admitted. "I'd rather you were out of my hair."

Scotty spoke softly to Gaylord. "Zee, get over to the *Examiner*. Have Frank Sanders send one of his boys down here right away. Tell him I'm real surprised at him, and if he don't print a retraction right away I'm gonna sue his ass for a million in libel for the damage he's done to my reppertation. That ought to repair our friendship good and tight."

Twenty minutes later bank president W.G. Fullerton's best eye was squinting through a magnifying lens, scrutinizing one of the sheets.

"Yerrrs. That's my signature, all right."

The duty sergeant pulled two big flat-irons out of Scotty's leather bag, and looked at them with a curious expression. "You're quite certain about that, Mr. Fullerton?"

73

"Yes, Sergeant. These bills are perfectly authentic. I sold the sheets to Mr. Scott myself."

Scotty grinned an I-told-you-so at Sheriff Ralphs. "You ever hear of a man printing money with two flat-irons Sheriff Ralphs?"

Ralphs was far from amused. He looked daggers at the Treasury man who had examined the sheet.

The Treasury official looked grudgingly over his wire-rimmed spectacles. "It was late, all right? The light was poor. So, I'm sorry. What do you want? Blood?"

The duty sergeant beamed. "I think you can go now, Mr. Scott."

"A deal is a deal, Sergeant. And I thank you."

As they started to troop off, reporters closed in, hunting quotes. But then, as they reached the door, Sheriff Ralphs laid a hand on Scotty's shoulder. He was evidently furious.

"Don't think I don't know what your game is, Scott."

"Just going about my lawful business, Sheriff Ralphs." Scotty smiled. "Is that a 'ph' or an 'f' in your last name? Only these newspaper people like to get things spelled right, don't you boys?"

The reporters began again to clamor for quotes as the Scotty circus moved outside. The reporters scribbled away and Ralphs stood his ground, but his anger frothed over like a shook-up soda and he yelled. "You set one foot wrong inside of San Bernardino County and you'll regret it. I'll teach you to make a fool out of me!"

"I don't need no lessons in how to do that." Scotty's smile broadened. "Anyhow, it seems to me you do a real good job all by yourself."

CHAPTER FIFTEEN

Los Angeles, California

LATER THAT DAY, in Jim Jeffries' Bar, Scotty was to be found celebrating. He was paying for drinks for a large group of hangers-on with a large pair of wall-paper shears and progressive slices of his uncut sheets. He had been recounting his experience to the listeners, who were all by now pretty well agog.

"So right then the Desk Sergeant opens up my bag and pulls out a couple of flat-irons, and he says to me, 'These must be the printing plates!' And I says, 'Sure they are – if you're wanting to counterfeit shirt collars, Sergeant!'"

Through the uproarious laughter came a familiar figure, still cast down, as was his way.

"Frank Sanders is real sore at you," Warner said, anxiously scanning for the newspaperman.

"Ha!" Scotty responded. "When you keep a coyote for a pet, you gotta think that someday he'll go wild on you."

Just then, the young newspaper seller crept in and pulled on Scotty's elbow. "News extra hot off the presses, Scotty!"

"Everybody – listen here – this is my good friend and business associate, Mr. Danny Mayer." Scotty told the room approvingly. "He is the very finest vendor of ephemeral literature this side of the Mississippi."

"What's wrong with the other side?" Danny piped up.

"Well, it ain't the side I'm standing on, so this must be the better side," Scotty said.

"I'll second that, Mr. Scott!"

"See what I mean?" Scotty beamed. "One day he's going to own half of this town, and the half he doesn't want he's gonna leave to me, ain'tcha?"

When Danny grinned, his teeth and the gaps between them showed like a castle battlement. He handed over a folded paper, accepted a dollar in return.

"I knew them ringtails got you figured all wrong in yesterday's edition, Scotty."

"Good boy! What did I always tell you about faith? This boy has faith! He'll go all the way. You could learn a little something from him, Zee."

Even Gaylord looked kind of chastened. Kate took the newspaper and opened it out.

"I never saw a newspaper article that apologized to anybody before," she said. "Scotty, look at it! You're completely exonerated"

Scotty did as he was bid, thinking it likely the best course where a woman was concerned. "Newspaper people ain't so hard to rope and tie – if you got 'em figured right. You just grab 'em by the horns, and down they go!" He turned around. "Bartender! Give me them scissors! Time to cut off another row of bills. Drinks all round!"

He flourished a bottle of champagne theatrically then bent down to pour some into a silver salver on the floor that served as a bowl for Windy.

"She doesn't like champagne," Kate said.

"I know, I know," Scotty told her quietly. "Windy's temperance: she don't drink alcohol at all. But Sam'll bring her some water directly."

As the rest of the gathering crowd gathered and crowded towards the bar, Gaylord made his move. He took Scotty aside a little way and talked confidentially to him.

"I take it you're still interested in the deal we talked about?"

Scotty eyed him dubiously. "I seem to recall that *you* were the one who suffered a loss of courage right around breakfast time."

"You should have leveled with me all along."

"Like I say, it never hurts to know who your real friends are. The ones who'll stick by you."

Gaylord looked offended. "I put up your bail money, didn't I?"

Scotty patted his arm. "I guess you did at that. And it shows I'm worth five hundred bucks of your affection, at the least."

"Five hundred was all they asked!"

"And maybe that's just as well." But after a momentary pout flitted across his face, he said with decision, "Yeah, Zee, let's do it! If you want a train stunt, I'll give you a train stunt to end all train stunts!"

Gaylord seemed relieved to have pulled it out of the fire. That probably meant he had been working hard on the deal up until

76

Scotty's apparent capsize.

"In that case," he said, "you may as well announce it here and now. Strike while the iron's hot."

"You reckon?"

"I do." Gaylord winked and gave him an envelope, at the same time lowering his voice still further. "That's the ten – plus five more for expenses. Look after it."

Scotty winked back, took the envelope, folded it over and put it in his shirt pocket. "All right. You got yourself a deal."

All along Scotty had seen Kate watching him, and he smiled at her and rippled his fingers in a fond wave.

"I tell you," Gaylord said. "After this you'll be a national hero. You have Sanders and those people you know in Chicago eating right out of your hand."

Scotty got up on a chair. "All right, everybody! Gather round! I got an announcement to make!"

When everyone had focused in on him, he told them, "I guess by now that everybody in California has heard about my little train ride. Well, let me tell you, I enjoyed that train ride so much I just took it into my head to take another one. Folks, I'm gonna have Los Angeles hear the name of Walter E. Scott whether they like it or not! I'm gonna burn up this city for a whole week! And when I'm done I'm going to burn up Chicago too! I'm heading up to the Windy City! And I'm going to do it in record time! Forty-eight hours! Do you hear me?"

"But that's impossible!" someone said. "It takes three days."

Warner agreed. "Walter, Chicago's thousands of miles away!"

"Two thousand, two hundred sixty-five miles to be exact," Scotty told the room. "Four million railroad ties. And I'm gonna travel over each and every one of them. And I'm gonna do it faster than anyone ever did it before!"

Later that night Scotty and Kate went walking together along Hill Street to catch the night air. They wandered past Central Park, past a bunch of lit-up hotels and as far as Angel's Flight, then they came back along Grand, 4th and Olive. All the while Windy the dog mooched about not far ahead of them. It was a perfect night but Kate was troubled.

"Scotty, I can't go with you," she said flatly.

"Sure you can. I already told everybody you would."

She faced him. "And I told you. I have to work for a living."

"Serving in Hathaway's hat store for a mangy twelve bucks fifty a week?" Scotty said. "Tell them ringtails you just quit."

Kate sighed with frustration, like a woman does when she can't get across a perfectly simple point to a man. "It's not that easy. My job's important to me. Don't you see: it's my independence. And Mr. Hathaway's not a ringtail. When my father died, he didn't leave a cent. It was the only job I could get, and I was grateful to Mr. Hathaway for that."

Scotty shook his head. His eyes hunted the darkness beyond the streetlamps. "Kate, where's your ambition? You can't stay in Hathaway's hat shop your whole life. Don't you know what's on offer here? It's the opportunity of a lifetime. You'll be famous all across America, like a duchess or a Vaudeville star. You'll be *somebody*."

Kate looked into his eyes. "I don't want to be famous. And I already *am* somebody. At least to me. Oh, Scotty, I can't live like you do. I never will get used to it."

Scotty was suddenly solicitous, but he was still uncomprehending. "I don't understand what you mean," he admitted. "I surely don't."

Kate hid her face in her hands for a moment. "All that drinking and story-telling and tinsel. All those false people crowing around. They only want you for your money. Don't you see that?"

Scotty could not have looked more shocked if she had hit him about the cheeks with a wet fish. "Well, of course I see that."

Kate struggled to explain herself. "It's like you're a river that's always in spate. Always roaring through the rapids. I just – need to catch my breath. I need a quiet pool of still water."

Scotty's brow knit. "Oh, Kate! You got me all wrong. Can't you see? I'm a simple feller at heart. I just live by my four 'don'ts', and that's it."

"Your four *whats*?"

"My four 'don'ts'." He began to ticked them off for her. "Don't say nothing that will hurt anybody. Don't give advice – nobody will take it anyway. Don't complain. And, best of all, don't explain."

She smiled a bittersweet smile at him, then. He hugged her for it and they kissed. Then they walked on, hand in hand.

"I guess I will come along if you *really* want me to," she said, knowing she was probably making another unrecognized sacrifice.

Scotty beamed. "I *really* want you to."

That seemed to settle it. After a moment she asked, "What was it that Gaylord gave you in that envelope?"

"Oh, no!" Scotty said defensively. "I won't tell you that."

"Why not?"

"Well, like I said, 'don't explain'."

CHAPTER SIXTEEN

Los Angeles, Santa Fe Depot

SCOTTY TOOK KATE down to the offices of the Santa Fe Railroad. All the way he had been scattering silver dollars for people along the street to scramble for, so a considerable following turned up at the station with the inevitable reporters in attendance.

In full showman style he called Mr. John M. Murphy, the Santa Fe general manager, outside his office and over to the big route board that shows the Santa Fe system. More than a hundred people were goggling at it, and still more were joining the throng and craning their necks at the back of the crowd to see for themselves what all the commotion was about.

"Now listen here, Mr. Murphy," Scotty announced in his best loud voice. "I need to take my lady friend, Kate, here to meet some millionaires I happen to know. They're having a whoop-de-doodle up by the shores of Lake Michigan a week today, and I can't leave Los Angeles for five more days. I want to know: what are you gonna do about that?"

Murphy played his part. "Mr. Scott, the Chicago Limited takes 72 hours."

Scotty drew himself up. "Mr. Murphy, I don't want to hear about no 'limiteds'. I need to be in Chicago inside of 48 hours. Now – can Santa Fe do it or not?"

Murphy scratched at his bald spot and admitted, "Even the record between Los Angles and Chicago is 57 hours and 56 minutes. That was when Mr. Peacock, Vice President of the Carnegie Steel Company was on extremely urgent business and -"

Scotty interrupted him. "Didn't I just tell you: my friends are preparing to hold a party? They're going ahead, expecting me to be there. Can Santa Fe do it, or not?"

Murphy looked hard at the route map. "Mr. Scott, to better the current record by 12 hours – we'd have to take every scheduled train out of service, clear the system. It would need a dozen locomotives all ready and waiting. Half the route is over mountain divisions. Why we'd need to break the land speed record!"

Scotty was unbudging. "I asked you, Mr. Murphy: can Santa Fe do it, or not?"

Murphy rose to the occasion, full of fight now. "Mr. Scott! We have the track. We have the equipment. And, by Jingo, we have the men to do it too! Santa Fe can make a man travel faster than any human being on earth has ever traveled before!"

Scotty turned to the crowd. "That's all I wanted to know!"

Murphy also turned to the crowd, "But the cost to you, Mr. Scott, would be absolutely prohibitive."

Scotty laughed him to scorn. "Well, it don't prohibit me none."

He pulled two $5,000 bills out of his boot tops and slapped them into Murphy's hand, while the crowd gasped as one.

"That's five – and five is ten! Ten thousand dollars, Mr. Murphy. See to the arrangements, and I'll see *you* in five days time!"

CHAPTER SEVENTEEN

Los Angeles, Santa Fe Station

FIVE DAYS PASSED, then Sunday came around. The train the newspapers had been calling the 'Coyote Special' all week was waiting at the station. All was bedecked with red, white and blue, Scotty's trademark colors. A gravel voiced vendor was going up the platform shouting at the enormous crowd which had gathered for the send-off.

"Hot dawgs! Corn dawgs! Scotty dawgs!"

A bunch of college boys were by the barrier at the front of the crowd eagerly watching in straw boaters and stiff high collars. They hooted as Windy the dog trotted by wearing a special red commemorative collar with a gold locomotive pendant. The Santa Fe Station had laid on a barber shop quartet, and it was singing up a storm a little way along the platform. In front of it a long, red carpet had been rolled out.

Scotty walked along it with the shyly demure Kate at his side. They boarded the train and joined John M. Murphy and a couple of other railroad officials. Scotty was puffing on a General Arthur cigar in the open rear of the observation car. He was all set, waving and now and then flipping silver dollars out into the crowd. Then came the popping of champagne corks, and a toast and a few words of unnecessary introduction from Murphy before Scotty eagerly took center stage.

Scotty addressed himself to his reporters. "Gentlemen, I have a personal bet with Mr. Murphy, here, that his Santa Fe railroad can't make this run in less than 48 hours. For every minute he gets me there sooner, I'll pay him $100. And for every minute longer he'll pay me $100. Now what do you think of that?"

Clock struck 1 p.m. The train began to pull out of the station.

The big, mustached engineer sat up front like the captain of a battleship, his fireman behind him shoveling coal like fury. The locomotive blasted out steam and smoke like a salute as it passed the California Industrial Co.'s rolling mill and the Union Ironworks on Mateo St and then headed across the river. Sparks flew up from the big 80-inch wheels as the engine raced around curves and clattered over switches at staggering speed. Scotty gave out champagne every time the train stopped for coal and water. They roared through Barstow station 26 minutes ahead of schedule. The entire population seemed to have turned out to watch the Coyote Special run through.

Bagdad, The Needles and Peach Springs flashed by as darkness closed in. They pulled in to Flagstaff, Arizona, in the middle of the night, then on to Albuquerque and Las Vegas, New Mexico, *en route* for Dodge City where they were to reset their watches. Scotty gave out $100 bills each time an engineer was retired. Engine change-overs were accomplished in one minute flat. The trackside was lined with sightseers at every community. Farmers and small-town folk all along the route had read about the Coyote Special. A group of Indians came out on their Appaloosas dressed in their Sunday best to watch. Scotty and Kate sat in the wildly swaying Pullman as the train crossed the Rockies and vaulted across the timber trestle bridges that spanned the gorges. The conductor and other staff and the three inevitable reporters who were in attendance smiled nervously at intervals. For much of the time Windy the dog stood in the aisle, all four legs braced out against the violent movement of the car. Other than that, she slept watchfully on one of the upholstered seats.

As lunch danced around the table Scotty was full of confidence and regaling the reporters with stories of what mystery might have been locked in a chest hidden inside a safe in Riverside, or how they had named a town in Arizona after him – which they hadn't.

The dinner menu read:

Caviar sandwiches a la Death Valley

Porterhouse Steak Coyote,
2 inches thick and a Marvel of Tenderness

Squab on toast with bacon strips au Scotty

Ice Cream and Colored Trimmings

Cheese Coffee Cigars

At night they slept in bouncing beds – strapped in. Light from under the engine shone out across the prairies. Fire from the smokestack erupted like a volcano in the darkness. Even in the middle of the night people brought their children out to watch the Coyote Special thundering past and the sparks flying.

During one of the engine changes Scotty made a bee-line for the telegraph office and before a grinning crowd dictated a wire to President Teddy Roosevelt:

AN AMERICAN COWBOY IS COMING EAST ON A
SPECIAL TRAIN FASTER THAN ANY COWPUNCHER
EVER RODE BEFORE STOP

HOW MUCH SHALL I BREAK TRANSCONTINENTAL
RECORD BY STOP

They passed the good people of Hutchinson, Newton and Emporia on the way through the state of Kansas. Topeka, but not Atchison, going instead by Lawrence on the Kaw River. They crossed the mighty Missouri at breakneck speed, and then the even mightier Mississippi going hell-for-leather near the historic town of Fort Madison, Iowa.

Near Galesburg, Illinois, Scotty pulled up his sleeves and went forward, with a reporter in tow, to help coal the engine. The furnace was white hot, the noise tremendous. Everything on the footplate was vibrating fit to fall apart, but astonishingly it held together. Wind was blasting at them as they entered the long downgrade straight. The engineer pointed to a red mark on the big brass dial. The needle was shaking itself off its spindle, but Scotty could see the train was clocking 106 mph.

The engineer shouted, "We just broke the world speed record!"

And Scotty gave him a hundred bucks.

Finally they slammed into Dearborn Road Station, brakes squealing. The Coyote Special came to a standstill an inch from the buffers, as the band struck up. The cheering crowds were enormous. Overhead the big clock read six minutes short of noon, and Scotty and Kate were feted like royalty as they were welcomed and led down from the train by the Santa Fe Company president himself.

Kate smiled her coy smile and looked around as she hung onto Scotty's arm. He was waving his hat overhead and lapping up the adulation.

"Looks like the Santa Fe got me here ahead of time after all," he told the crowd. "I guess I owe Mr. Murphy a couple thousand bucks, but it was worth it!"

Scotty patted his dog, and she looked up at him with the kind of expectation that only a border collie can show.

"Look it, Windy!" he said. "They even named this city after you."

A reporter called out. "Why did you do it, Mr. Scott?"

"For the fun of it! Why else?"

"How do you feel, Mr. Scott?"

"It's just downright Western exuberance. The world is too small for the kind of whoop I want to give!"

They had taken the very best suite at the Northwestern Hotel, and the biggest room was full of well-wishers' flowers and reporters and photographers. A man with a cap on the wrong way round was hand-cranking a movie camera as a crew of big-wig railroad officials and local dignitaries posed.

"A mighty fine city, Chicago! Mighty fine!" Scotty opined, but then found himself distracted by a room service boy. "Now you tell 'em Krug. Vintage Krug. Got that?" He tucked a bill into the boy's jacket and turned back. "Always be kind to the hired help, that's what I always say. Could be you or me, and used to be once."

The reporters scribbled furiously.

To Kate, he said quietly, "You feeling all right, my dear?"

Kate gave a brave smile, she looked exhausted, and as if she just wanted to put her feet up.

"I'm fine. Really I am."

"Better make this the last picture, boys," Scotty said.

There was a photographic rush as they got up and posed again.

"Say, fellers! How long is it to New York from here?"

"By train?" one of the reporters asked.

"What other possible way is there to travel?" Scotty asked, shooting a glance at the Santa Fe's general manager.

"Oh, eighteen hours."

"Can't nobody sell me a ticket for thirteen?" He brandished his bankroll. "Better tell those boys in New York I have $100,000 for any steamship line will get me to Southampton, England, inside of five days. America needs speed. That's what this new century's all about." He turned to the youngest reporter. "Write that down just like I said it."

Their waiter brought in a tray of drinks. Scotty peeled off $100 bills, made a great show out of finding a lousy $10 bill hiding in there. He picks it out like was a fly in his ointment, screwed it up and threw it away. He gave the hundred to the eight-dollars-fifty-a-week waiter, whose eyes almost popped out of their sockets.

"Keep the change. Like I say, boys, you never know what tomorrow will bring."

A little way across town, Johnson was propped up in his chair reading a dime Western – *The Rustlers of Laramie Falls* – when Garrett entered brusquely, trailed by Johnson's visibly affronted butler.

"'If I was you I'd keep a tight rein on my investments, Jimmy,'" Garrett quoted with a good deal of sarcasm.

He thrust the newspaper at Johnson, who read, and as he read his face changed color. The front page was filled with news of Walter E. Scott's train extravaganza. A fear of trains had never really left him, and he marveled at the idea of breaking the world speed record aboard one of them. Scott really must have *cojones* of steel.

Having spent all his sarcasm, Garrett attempted aggressive irony. "So giving him a third stake will keep him working, will it?"

Johnson's own attempt was at total mystification. "I don't know what he's up to."

"Neither do I, Albert, but whatever it is, it isn't gold mining!"

"No ... I suppose it's not."

Garrett's anger moderated to exasperation. He had no idea how to handle this man, which was unusual. Eventually he flopped uninvited into an armchair and said, "I'd have him shot – but unfortunately he's too famous for that now."

Johnson pursed his lips. "No. I think there's a better way."

Garrett scowled. "How much will it cost, this time?"

"Jim, where's he getting the money to charter express trains?" He shrugged. "There *has* to be a Peerless Mine."

Bessie entered with a maid in tow. An ominous cup was on her tray.

"Albert, it's time for your hot milk."

Johnson looked daggers at the cup, then said to Garrett, "There's only one way to find out once and for all. I'm going out there myself!"

Bessie drew in a horrified breath. "Out *where*, Albert?"

Johnson said definitely: "Out West."

"But ... you can't do that!"

"Why not?"

"Because ... Albert ... think about your back."

Johnson, roused now, got unsteadily to his feet. "That's just what I intend to quit thinking about for once. To Hell with my damned back!"

CHAPTER EIGHTEEN

Los Angeles, the Lankershim Hotel

SCOTTY STOOD AT the door of his suite, holding out the telegram to Warner who was even more anxious than was usual for him.

"He's gonna do *what*?" Warner asked.

"He's coming out here." Scotty slapped the telegram with the back of his hand then turned to the telegram boy. "Ever see silver come out of a gold mine, son?"

"No, sir."

Scotty dropped a five dollar coin into the boy's hand. "Well, now you did."

"Thank you, Mr. Scott!"

Scotty called after the boy. "Don't drink it all at once."

"Johnson's coming to Los Angeles?" Warner gulped. "But you told me he couldn't so much as get out of bed."

"He said he was laid up six months after he broke his back. He kinda hobbles around some now. He's the unhealthiest man I ever did clap eyes on. Said he had a fear of train travel too. Not surprising, given that it killed his Daddy and damned near did for him too."

"I told you you shouldn'ta gone to Chicago on that train. Now look what a nest of hornets you stirred up! I suppose Garrett's coming out too."

"Nope. But he's sending out a mining engineer. Feller by the name of Brighton."

Warner was aghast to the point of lapel-pulling, but then it never took much to work him up. "He'll want you to show him the mine! What you gonna do?"

Scotty smiled. "I'll have to think on that a while."

Later that day in a low down bar at the bottom of East 6th St, Scotty was pouring 'Millionaire Bill' a drink and tucking a hundred into his top pocket. Bill produced an amiable, if toothless, smile. Bill enjoyed intrigue and Scotty was becoming increasingly conspiratorial.

"Bill, you know I'll be damned if I'm gonna show anyone where my mine is!"

"That's wise, Scotty. There ain't no such thing as a shared secret."

"So – if it comes to it – I'll just have to show them yours."

Millionaire Bill smiled again and went along with it. "You are welcome. But thain't nothing much in it no more. All there was I already dug out and spent."

"Which is why I got another plan." Scotty pulled his stool up closer. "Here's what you do. You and Bob Peg Leg get up on the ridge right up by Wingate Wash and hide out good. Then you wait for us to come by. You got that?"

Bill confirmed vaguely what he'd been told, then said, "There'll be you, uh – Mr. Johnson, Mr. Brighton ... and ...?"

"And Warner."

"Oh, yeah. That misery guts brother of yours."

Scotty nodded solicitously. "Right. Now, I'll be riding my mule up ahead. Johnson has a bad back so he can't ride. Warner will be up alongside him driving a four-mule rig. Brighton will be on another mule. Now as soon as you see the rig come by on the track below you crank off a couple of rifle shots. You got that?

"A couple of rifle shots," Bill repeated. "I would gladly do that for you, Scotty. Only ..."

"Only?"

"I ain't got me a rifle no more. And Bob Peg Leg ain't got no rifle neither."

"You can take my Mauser."

"Does it shoot good?"

"Straight as a die."

Bill sucked his gums. "Suppose ... suppose those fellers don't scare."

Scotty chuckled. "Are you kidding me? Johnson's back was broke once in a train wreck. After three days jolting on a Death Valley track and three nights sleeping on hard ground he'll be looking for any excuse to get the hell out of there."

"He will at that."

"And you can bet that all the way up from Barstow I'll be telling them the most blood-curdlin' bandit stories I can think of."

89

"Ooo-eee. They'll be rattled like rats in a cage, Scotty."
"I'm thinking so, Bill. I'm thinking so."

CHAPTER NINETEEN

Near Death Valley

IT WAS THE second day out and the party were camping at Lone Willow Spring near China Lake. Darkness was coming on. The tent was already pitched, and Warner was unloading supplies from the rig. Windy was chewing on a shank bone brought along specifically for her comfort. Brighton was sat on a rock, shucking off his boots and massaging his feet.

Scotty toe poked one of Brighton's boots. "Didn't I tell you to keep your boots on out here?"

Brighton looked up all resentful and sore. "But this is camp."

"Tell it to the rattlers. They don't know that."

Warner looked around, scratching his pate. "I'm right sorry, Mr. Johnson, but I was sure I packed up those canvas beds back in Barstow. I can't think how they got left behind."

Johnson breathed deep and scanned the far hills. "Never mind about that on my account. I have to sleep on a hard surface back at home anyhow. It won't hurt me to lie on the ground."

Scotty folded his arms uncompromisingly. "You got to watch out for scorpions. The little ones are the killers. I know a half-Paiute feller name of Bob Peg-Leg got himself stung on the big toe by one of them nasty little chiggers. He was alone out here and he had to cut his own leg off to save his life."

Brighton grunted in an I-don't-believe-that-for-a- second sort of way.

"What?" Scotty challenged.

"I don't believe that for a second," Brighton said, showing he was a forthright sort of man.

"I'm telling you," Scotty told him. "And lucky he did cut it off. Or he would have been known around here as Bob Stone Dead." He called to Warner. "Warner – ain't that right?"

Warner nodded. "Uh? Oh – yeah."

Scotty turned back to Brighton. "Anyhow, you seen Bob Peg Leg yourself. Back at Barstow station."

"You mean that Indian who helped unload our gear?"

"That's the feller. Half Cherokee."

91

Brighton reluctantly pulled his left boot back on. "I bet he's the one stole our camp beds." After a moment he said, "Anyhow I thought you said he was half Paiute."

"I did. Two halves make a whole, don't they? Half of him's Paiute and the other half's Cherokee. And just because he's an Indian it don't mean he's a thief."

Johnson was standing a little way apart, hands on hips, breathing deeply. "Hmmmm ... just smell that air. It's like wine."

Scotty looked to him, wondering that he seemed to have found a kindred soul, but aware also that things were not going according to plan so far as Johnson was concerned.

Brighton said irritably, "Can't you light a fire so we can fix some hot food?"

Scotty looked sharply to him. "And risk bringing the bandits down on us?"

"What bandits?"

Scotty blew out a big breath that showed he didn't think much of Brighton's desert craft. "I guess you don't know. The hills hereabouts are swarming with all kinds of n'er-do-wells."

Brighton said. "I can easily believe that."

"Jupiter and Mars," Johnson said, looking up into the purple velvet sky. "And a day-old moon like a fingernail paring. It makes a man feel at one with the universe."

Scotty went over to the mules. He made a fuss of one of them, and it responded to him. Johnson turned and hobbled towards him. He said, "You know, Scotty, this is the first time my nose has stopped running in six months."

Scotty refolded his arms. "You want to be careful about breathing in too much of that borax dust when we get down into the Valley. It makes a poisonous mess of a man's innards."

"I can smell things again," Johnson said blithely. "My cough's gone too. This hot, dry air works just like a cure. I ought to bottle it and sell it as lung medicine."

Scotty thought he couldn't let that notion go unscathed. "You wouldn't talk like that if you'd seen the dust storms that come over these hills. I seen men buried right where they slept. And when them dusters come on they don't give no warning on ya."

He began tickling the mule affectionately.

92

"Fine animal," Johnson said.

"You're right there. Nobody much knows what a fine animal a mule is. Hardy. Intelligent. Friendly. And they know a whole lot, most of them. They got a reppertation for being stubborn, but there ain't no such thing as a bad mule – only a stupid owner."

"You like animals, don't you?"

Scotty's chin jutted. "Treat animals fair and they'll love you. They don't care what you say, it's what you do that counts with animals. Not like most dumb people. And these judy's have got horses beat a mile. Look it. The only beast of burden that thrives out here. I'm telling you. This one right here's my favorite. I call him Slim."

Johnson made a big decision. "Scotty, tomorrow, I'd rather like to try riding him. If I may?"

Scotty put his fingers to his chin and appraised Johnson afresh. Concern for his wobbling plan was being slowly overcome by an inner delight that Johnson appeared to share respect for the things that he himself valued. Who would have thought it?

"If you think your spine can take it – well, that's fine with Slim." Scotty looked at the mule again and nodded. "So I guess it's fine with me."

Later that night all four men were under their blankets and huddled on the ground. They were not yet asleep. Brighton's jaw was set, his face grimly thoughtful. Warner was on his side, staring glumly into the dust. Johnson was flat on his back, his hands laced together back of his head. He was staring up at the firmament, which was brightly vivid. Scotty's face had mischief in it as out from under the blanket he pulled a rattlesnake rattle. He glanced towards the heavens, then shook it.

He stopped and listened. Silence. Then he shook it again a little more vigorously. This time he heard Brighton say, "Uh!"

Scotty, in a ferocious whisper, said, "Keep still!"

"What is it?"

"Nothing to worry about."

Brighton began to worry.

Then two very loud shots rang out accompanied by two stabs of brilliant light in the darkness.

"Aggh!" Brighton said.

Both Warner and Johnson stirred at this, but Scotty calmed them.

"Don't worry. Just turn right over and go back to sleep," he said. Then he added, "I missed the scaly sonofabitch, but he probably won't think to bother us again tonight."

The next day, high among the desert hills, Bob Peg Leg lay slumped down behind a breastwork of rocks that overlooked the narrow pass below. Hunkered down beside Bob was Millionaire Bill, Scotty's Mauser '98 rifle propped up right by his elbow. Bill was looking morose and strangely glassy-eyed. The sun was glaring bright, there was no shade and it was incredibly hot. Bill burped loudly.

Bob sipped from a canteen of warm water and seemed calmly at ease.

"How long we been up here?" he asked. "Bill? You sure it was supposed to be today?"

Bill was slow to rouse himself to the question, and when he did his head floated round in a groggy way.

"Hmmmmmmmmm?"

Bob showed his disapproval. He crawled over to pick up Bill's quart canteen. He rattled it, revealing that it was almost empty. When he unstoppered it and sniffed, he recoiled from the fumes."

"Oh, Bill ... now I am disappointed in you. A quart of whisky?" Bob Peg Leg blew out a breath. "That's no way for a white man to eat breakfast on a working day."

It was coming up to noon at Wingate Pass, and Johnson was up on his mule, riding. Stiffly, Scotty thought, but he was doing all right. Warner was up on the wagon with Brighton beside him.

Scotty rode out front about a hundred yards on his second mule until he came abreast of a neat pile of rocks and a sign that read:

WINGATE PASS (ELEVATION 1,976 FT)

SAN BERNARDINO COUNTY | INYO COUNTY

He turned the mule around and cantered back, holding his hand

94

up.

"Whoa!"

Scotty trotted up to the now stationery rig. All the jocularity of last night was gone from him.

"I want you all to keep together," he said.

Johnson blinked at him. "Anything wrong?"

Scotty's eyes scanned the heights enigmatically. "Just a feeling. We're about to enter Death Valley, Mr. Brighton."

The atmosphere was suddenly tense. Scotty took out one of the two .30 caliber rifles they had in the wagon.

Brighton said, "What are you doing?"

"Just a precaution. There's no cause for alarm."

Johnson was wary. "What have you seen?"

Scotty continued to stare at the hills. "Injuns. But don't let the thought of a party of bloodthirsty savages scare you. I recommend we continue right on. Whatever the risk."

Brighton's eyes narrowed. His cynicism was equal to the gambit. "Mr. Scott, you're pushing at an open door. Now let's just get along, shall we?"

At that moment a rifle bullet crashed into the wagon's side, splintering off the wood. A half second later the rifle report reached them. Johnson's mule bucked and he was thrown heavily to the ground. Scotty's reaction was one of horror. He was suddenly galvanized to action. But the mules in the traces were spooked, and as Warner struggled to control the rig, the sudden bolting threw Brighton backward heels-over-head so he landed in the back of the wagon.

Another shot rang out, and this time it hit Warner, who let go the reins. In agony, he grabbed at his left thigh and rolled off the wagon seat.

Scotty was cantering forward, waving his arms to stop the firing. He looked over his shoulder to where Brighton was lifting himself up.

Three more rifle shots rang in rapid succession.

"Get down!" Scotty yelled.

He kicked the mule along the track a little way, almost as far as the neat pile of rocks where the signpost stood, and then he fired off a couple of rounds of his own into the hills.

Scotty hollered, "Quit it! Warner's hit! Stop shooting!"

Up on the breastwork Millionaire Bill, crazy with drink, continued shooting wildly. A false leg appeared and then came down on the crown of Bill's head. He dropped the rifle and disappeared. Then Bob – for obvious reasons – overbalanced backwards and disappeared too.

Warner was lying in a pool of blood. Johnson had come up to him as Scotty reached them and leapt down from the mule.

"He's shot in the leg," Johnson observed.

Warner, scared out of his wits by the blood, said, "Ahhhh! I'm gonna die! I'm gonna die!"

Scotty shouted at him with the fury of fear. "You're not gonna die, Goddamn you! Let me look." Then he said, "Oh, sweet Jesus ..."

Warner didn't like that. "What?" he said. "Is it bad?"

Scotty told Johnson, "We gotta stop the bleeding!"

But Johnson was shaking his head, shocked and nonplussed for the moment. It was amazing to him how quickly and how suddenly everything had turned into a nightmare. But he snapped out of it just as fast. He unfolded a little city pocket-knife and slit Warner's trouser leg up past the knee. Then he cut off the fabric and twisted it into a rope.

"Fetch me a stick," he told Scotty.

When Scotty only stared, horrified by the wound in his brother's leg, Johnson repeated the order.

"Fetch me a stick! I need to make a tourniquet."

Scotty came to his senses. He broke a dry stick off a scrub bush and Johnson set to work shutting off the blood flow. All the while Warner was groaning and mumbling.

"I told you, you're not going to die," Scotty told him.

Johnson looked up. "What now?"

"I'll run down the rig. We gotta get him to a doctor."

Johnson agreed. "His color's still high. Looks like the bullet's still in there, though. You're right he needs help."

Scotty jumped back aboard Slim and galloped off to where the rig has come to a stop. Brighton was in the back. His cynical composure had disappeared. When he saw Scotty he jumped up from the bed of the wagon, clutching a knife and yelled ferociously. He was terrified and still believed he was under attack from blood thirty bandits.

Scotty told him frankly, "Warner's hit bad. I'm fearful he might die. We gotta get him out of here quick."

CHAPTER TWENTY

Los Angeles – Mercy Hospital

THE DOORS BURST open and in came Scotty with Johnson right behind him. Nurses in starched uniforms were in attendance. Scotty was met by Dr. Kilgore, an unsmiling, weasel-eyed man of about fifty-five, with oiled, thin white hair center-parted. He wore half-moon spectacles with wire frames. He took a dim view of the intrusion by what seemed to be a couple of dust-crusted desert down and outs.

Scotty was anxious. "Doctor – it's my brother. He's hurt real bad."

Outside was a bone shaker with Warner on a stretcher in back. Warner looked deathly pale. Kilgore looked him over cursorily.

"Gunshot wound?"

"Yeah."

"What do you want me to do about it?

Scotty goggled. "Why, fix him up. You're a doctor, ain't you?"

"When will you people learn that playing with guns is liable to get you killed?" Kilgore said icily. "Which of you did it?"

"Neither of us! It was an accident!"

"It always is – with your type. Was he drunk?"

"It was two days ago. He's lost a lot of blood."

"Two days? Is he insured?"

"*What*?"

Johnson stepped forward. "Yes. Yes he is."

Kilgore peered over his eye-glasses at Johnson. He did not seem disposed to believe him.

Johnson offered an ingratiating but nevertheless tight smile. "He's insured with National Life of Chicago."

"Well, I need to see his policy."

Scotty pleaded. "Please, I'll give you anything you want if you'll just save my brother's life."

"Mister," Kilgore said, "this is not a charity hospital. The cost of care here could easily run to a hundred dollars or more."

Scotty could hardly believe his plan had come to this. "Doc, there's no occasion for him to die. It's only money. I'll give you a thousand dollars if you want it."

Johnson said, "And I'll guarantee that offer."

Kilgore gave them both a withering look.

Scotty burst out, "I don't need any guarantees! Listen: I own the Peerless gold mine. I'm Death Valley Scotty."

"Yes," Kilgore agreed. "And I'm the Queen of Sheba."

"But you must have heard of me!"

"I'm afraid I have not."

Two hospital porters were standing by. One of them nodded and said, "He *is* Death Valley Scotty. I seen his picture."

"Doc, I'll give you a thousand dollars in cold cash if you him alive."

Kilgore hesitated, then nodded to the hospital porters. "I suppose you'd better bring the man inside."

Johnson was sitting on a waiting room bench seat. Scotty was standing with his back to him, looking out the window. Agony was in the air.

Scotty asked, "What's Brighton gonna say when he gets back to Chicago?"

Johnson looked across. "That he isn't being paid enough to do the job Jim Garrett wants him to do."

"I can understand that."

Scotty put his face in his hands, then looked up to the high ceiling where two flies chased each other with amazing persistence around a stationary fan. "I'm sorry about what happened out there."

"Yes," Johnson said quietly. "I know you are."

Just then, a nurse came by.

"Mr. Scott? The surgeon has sewn up your brother's leg. It's taken twenty-six stitches."

"Will he live?"

"I'm afraid the bullet is still lodged in there. It'll have to be removed, but we can't operate again for a day or two."

"That ain't what I asked you."

Johnson said placatingly, "Looks like Warner's going to be all right."

"Well, I hope so."

"And with a bit of luck, he might even forgive you."

Scotty looked askance suddenly. "What do you mean? It wasn't *me* who was responsible."

"No," Johnson said simply. "I guess you weren't."

Scotty went back to ruminating and staring out the window, but then a voice he half recognized said: "Who was *responsible* is what a jury is gonna decide."

Scotty turned, and was shocked to see none other than John C. Ralphs, Sheriff of San Bernardino County. There was undisguised satisfaction on the man's face, and a nickel-plated pistol in his hand.

"Sheriff Ralphs."

"The very same," Ralphs admitted. "And I am a hard lawman who hates the flim-flam of people like you. I am also steely in pursuit. I might warn you that if you are considering jumping out of that window two other lawmen are with me."

"I have no such plans."

Ralphs took out his trusty handcuffs. "I told you to stay out of my county, Walter Scott. I have here a telegraphic warrant for your arrest. The charge is conspiracy to murder."

Johnson stood up as Kate came to meet him. It was a few mornings later and they were in the lobby of the Hotel Lankershim.

"Scotty says thank you very much for standing his bail," Kate said.

"It was a five hundred dollar bond. But worth it to get him out." He looked toward the elevators. "So – where is he?"

"I'm afraid he's not here."

"Not here?"

"He says to tell you he's sorry he can't meet you, but he has something important to do today."

Johnson looked past her anxiously. "Well, I like *that*!"

"Mr. Johnson, he does send his apologies. He said what he had to do was urgent."

"Well, I'll be a son of a -" Johnson stopped himself, showed his exasperation by slapping his hat against his leg, but he just about maintained his good manners. "Excuse me."

Kate searched his face. "Are you all right? ... Mr. Johnson?"

Johnson mastered his frustration. "It's just ... Scotty and I have a train to catch."

Kate blinked, mystified. "A train?"

"The train to Barstow. I came here to visit Death Valley with Scotty, and that's what we're going to do. Whether he likes it or not."

Kate disliked being caught in the middle of things, so she tried to be helpful. "Well, Scotty said not to mention it to you, but ... I believe he's gone to visit Warner."

Johnson's face darkened further. "Oh, he *has*, has he?"

"Don't think badly of him," Kate said. "You see, Warner's having the bullet removed from his leg today."

The last of Johnson's irritation fell suddenly away. "Well, I suppose compassion counts as a sufficient excuse."

"Mr. Johnson, about Scotty. You know, I've fallen for him in the worst way, but I can't help feeling ... well, he's just not like anybody I've ever met."

Johnson smiled, touched by her innocence. "You can say that again."

"What I mean to say is: is there anything you know about him that you think I ought to know?"

"My dear, I'm going to have to re-arrange these train tickets. If you'll accompany me to the station, I'll tell you everything I know about the man."

CHAPTER TWENTY-ONE

Hewes Market, Los Angeles

WHAT KATE SHOULD have known but did not, was that, at that very moment Scotty was standing on the sidewalk three blocks away at Hewes Market. He'd been at a butcher's counter buying a side of beef, and had planned to haul it back to the hotel in a car.

Twenty minutes later, and that plan had worked beautifully. He paid off the driver, heaved the beef across his shoulder, carried it through the lobby and into the hotel elevator, which he ascended alongside a bewildered old lady.

Scotty affected a smile. "I'm feeling a mite peckish," he told her.

The old lady stared straight ahead, both hands firmly on her umbrella handle. Nobody wants to make reply to an obvious nut.

Once at his floor Scotty dragged the beef to his room and as soon as he had it inside he threw it onto the bed, locked the door and pulled out a Springfield rifle. He wrapped blankets around the barrel, pointed it at the beef and fired into the meat.

The noise was loud but muffled, and not way out of line with the occasional backfires that came up from the traffic passing below along 7th.

After Scotty laid the rifle aside he began to search inside the meat with his finger. Then he used a pocket knife worked his way down. Eventually, he came up with what he was looking for: a squashed bullet.

By a quarter after two, Scotty was prowling the corridors of Mercy hospital. He spotted a nurse going about her trade and stopped her.

"Excuse me," he said. "Could you tell me where Warner Scott is?"

The nurse smiled at him. "Why – he's in surgery right now."

"Which room would that be?"

"He's in the John Hunter Memorial Operating Theater. It's right along there, but you'd best wait here."

Scotty smiled a 'thank you' and went to sit down. As soon as the nurse had gone, he crept towards a pair of doors, cracked them slightly ajar and took a peek into what lay beyond.

Inside, the operating theater all was hustle and bustle. It really was a theater, Scotty decided. Not one with a stage and a lot of dancing girls, but maybe like a college lecture theater. It smelled peculiar, like carbolic soap being boiled up in a gin still. Sitting up on the steep gallery of seat, watching, were a bunch of medical students, all of them wearing white coats. They were taking notes. Warner was down on the slab out cold with a pad of white gauze piled on his face, Surgeon Kilgore and a couple of masked and gowned assistants were bent over his etherated form.

It was perfect, Scotty decided. He had arrived, most fortuitously, in the nick of time.

Scotty scouted around and found a small janitor's wash-room. He took a grubby white coat from off a peg and saw a couple of books on a table. "*A New Course in Electricity*" and "*Modern Heating and Ductwork Vol. II.*" Not ideal, but they would just have to do. He picked them up and stepped back the way he had come. It was no matter to slink into one of the rows of seating near the back of the room and take his place.

He looked down at the proceedings with a grimace on his face as Kilgore's voice floated up. Warner's leg was now laid wide open, and a running commentary was being given by Kilgore for the benefit of those who had come to learn the mysteries of the human form and how to heal its hurts. It was more a matter of horrified fascination to Scotty. It wasn't that he was unduly squeamish about blood, it was just that you simply couldn't regard a sibling's wounds in the same way you regarded a stranger's. That was a fact.

"In this case," Kilgore explained in his high-falutingest voice, "the projectile entered here, just under the superior end of the *musculus sartorius*, damaging the *quadriceps femoris* here ... and here."

Back in row four, Scotty nodded sagely.

"A few inches higher," Kilgore went on, making an attempt at mild dark humor, "and the patient's local church choir would have been looking forward to welcoming a new soprano."

A ripple passed among the students, then they looked on again with absorbed attention. No one noticed as Scotty slid forward to the third, then the second, then the front row and studiously opened at page 137: "*Chapter Eight – Alternating Current.*" When Kilgore looked up, Scotty looked down, and put his hand to his brow as if mulling over some intractable problem of anatomy.

"There was extensive damage to the *abductor longus* and the various branches of the *nervus femoralis*, Kilgore went on. "In other words, gentlemen, it must have hurt like hell."

There was another ripple of amusement.

Kilgore quelled it by moving in closer on the leg. "Fortunately, at this point the *arteria femoralis* and *vena femoralis* run parallel, and only the latter sustained slight damage – which was nevertheless sufficient to cause extensive loss of blood. This made it impossible to remove the projectile when the patient was first admitted."

An assistant in a gauze mask used an atomizer to drench the wound with a carbolic spray.

"The bone has been chipped here at the superior process, and it is here that the projectile is located." Kilgore turned to his other assistant. "Forceps, if you please." He took the instrument and dubiously at his handiwork. "I am now going into the wound to retrieve the projectile."

Scotty knew that his face must be pale and spangled with sweat. The whole healing process was making him feel distinctly ill. Below the bench his fingers were nervously polishing the slug he had removed from that unlucky side of beef.

A groan from Warner down on the table prompted Dr. Kilgore to say, "Mr. Taylor, more ether, please."

More of the aromatic fluid dripped onto the cotton lint pad that covered Warner's nose and mouth, and the flickering of his eyeballs behind their closed lids stilled again.

Close by was an empty kidney-shaped white enamel dish. Then, a moment later, a bloody bullet held in steel forceps appeared over the dish and was released. It dropped into the dish with a leaden sound.

Kilgore said, "There we are, gentlemen: mission accomplished. Now we close the wound first by suturing the fibers of the *adductor longus*. Note there has been remarkably little evidence of infection in the muscle tissue. This is due to our sterile procedures ..."

Behind Kilgore, the surgical assistant carried the white enamel dish to a wheeled trolley that stood to one side of the auditorium. It contained a variety of used instruments. Underneath it was a bucket.

Scotty retched, covered his mouth with his hand and stumbled out towards the operating table.

Kilgore, hardly looking up from his stitching, said, "There's always one, isn't there?" Then more forcefully he called out, "Not on the floor, man! In the bucket!"

Scotty veered toward the trolley. As he reached it he vomited over the bucket. His hand went into the dish, and he swapped the bloodied bullet for the one he had brought with him.

His own mission accomplished, he left the theater just as fast as he could.

That night, in a low down bar at the bottom of East 6th St, Scotty was pouring Millionaire Bill a drink. Bill was scared and guilty and pathetically apologetic about having shot Warner. But Scotty had decided he was going to be in a forgiving mood, whether or not it was what Warner would have wanted.

"You won't tell them where I am, willya?" Bill pleaded. He was still shaken up. This was the first time he had nearly murdered anybody.

Scotty set the tumbler of rye down in front of Bill. "Don't worry, partner. I got it all in hand."

But Bill remained inconsolable. "I'm sorry, Scotty. I didn't mean to do it. I just didn't know what I was doing ..."

"Not so loud, Bill."

Bill jolted as he recollected himself. "Sorry, Scotty," he whispered.

"You are forgiven. Look –"

He held up the swapped bullet between finger and thumb.

"What's that?" Bill said as if a new horror was about to start plaguing him.

"It's the one thing that connects you and me with the ambush. Everybody knows my rifle's a Mauser '98. That shoots 7.92 millimeter." He winked and lowered his voice still further. "This is the slug that come out of Warner's leg. The one the police got was shot out of a Springfield."

"Scotty ..."

Scotty poked Bill playfully in the shoulder. "I know, I know. You're sorry. We're all sorry. But you can make amends by keeping your trap shut. You got that?"

"But what about Warner? When he wakes up, he'll talk for sure."

The Mercy Hospital smelled clean and fresh and the starched uniforms of its many nurses were a reassuring sight to anyone who believed that germs and sick people ought not to mix.

Scotty and Kate walked through the ward towards Warner's bed. Scotty was carrying a brown paper sack.

"The doc says he's gonna be just fine," Scotty said. "He just has to lie there a while and 'cuperate up a little."

Kate had still not settled in her own mind what she was eventually going to think about the incident, so a reservation of judgment seemed the proper course. She had showed her suspicions, along with more than a little disapproval, and it had produced an unexpected meekness in the man.

"You were lucky you weren't all killed," she chided. "I get so worried when you leave town. There must be some very unsavory characters out in that desert. And you're bound to attract trouble the way you go on."

"It wasn't quite like that."

"Did you see Mr. Johnson?"

Scotty made a face. "He's still hanging around, waiting on me to take him out to Death Valley."

"Will you do it?" she asked. "He knows very well you've been trying to avoid him."

"You think so?"

"I know so."

"What do *you* think I should do?"

"You promised, so you should take him."

Scotty took a deep breath of disinfected air and said, "Well, then, I will. I would have gone before, It's just I had a little business to clear up first."

They came to Warner's room and approached the bed. The injured brother was not exactly pleased to see the uninjured one.

"Warner – how you feeling? I brung you some grapes. I know you like the black ones best. See."

Warner had his arms folded across his chest.

"Kate," he said, "tell him he can take his grapes and – and eat them in his own good time. In the meantime he can oblige me by getting out of my sight!"

Kate was taken aback at this. "Don't you think you're being a little ungrateful?" she demanded. "After all, he did save your life. And he's put up a thousand dollars of his own money so you can get the best attention."

A certain redness began to suffuse Warner's face. "Is that's what you told her? Is it? That you saved my life? Devil take you, Walter, you are a prize romancer! You really are!"

"Warner, can't you try to see it from my point of view just once?"

"No, no! You see it from *my* point of view for once. Look at me, Walter. I'm crippled. Damn near killed. I should never have listened to you for a minute."

Kate said, "Warner – it was an accident."

Warner looked pityingly at her. "Is that what he said?" He turned to Scotty. "Is that what you told her?" His point made, he turned back. "Kate, you don't know nothing about it! It was all a put-up thing."

Scotty said quickly, "Now nobody meant for you to get shot."

"Then how come I am shot? When we was kids it was always me who picked up the licking for your wild schemes. Well, you're gonna pay this time. You betcha!"

Scotty picked up his hat and stood up. "Come on, Kate. He ain't in no mood to talk sense."

They beat a retreat but Warner called after them, "And I ain't ever gonna be in a mood to talk to you again. Not ever! You better get yourself a real good lawyer!"

As they rounded the corner, Kate said "What did he mean by that?"

"Don't worry," Scotty told her. "He'll come around. He always does."

"And Mr. Johnson?"

"He's a man who needs avoiding right now."

"Scotty, you promised."

And her eyes were so wide and so endlessly deep that he sighed and said, "I guess I did, didn't I."

107

CHAPTER TWENTY-TWO

Death Valley

THREE PAIUTES WERE were standing on the high bluff, watching the road below. On the rocks behind them were ancient rock drawings – one shaped like a human hand. Death Valley was their land, but it was as if they were sadly waving goodbye to it.

Down below, Scotty and Johnson were on mules. Other mules followed, loaded with baggage. Windy was tagging along. Despite his forebodings, Scotty was in amiable mood and halfway through a tale.

"... and then, after that, I worked as water boy for a survey team that come down here. I was naught but eleven years old. And after that I worked as swampier on them big twenty-mule teams that used to haul borax up out of the Valley. We come along this very track. That was hot work. I used to sit up on the wagons all day and just ... dream."

Johnson's reaction was that of a man evaluating another piece of evidence that was leading him slowly toward the proof of a theory.

"What was it you dreamed about?" he asked.

Scotty grinned. "Oh, you'd laugh if I told you."

"No, I wouldn't."

"Yes, you would."

"I wouldn't. You shouldn't be scared that I'll laugh. So what, if anyone laughs at you?" Johnson waited for that to sink in, then he said, "All right then, don't tell me, if you don't want to."

Scotty took a deep breath. "No, I will. I will ... I used to look up at those mountains over there and dream that one day I'd live in a castle in amongst 'em."

Johnson showed his surprise, but that fell short of a laugh. "A castle?"

"Yup."

"What kind of a castle?"

Scotty shrugged. "You know. Just a regular castle. Like they got in Spain and elsewhere. That was my dream anyhow."

"Just a regular castle, huh?"

Scotty "See – I knew you'd laugh at me."

Johnson, laughing now, said, "I'm not laughing. I think it's a wonderful idea. Splendid!"

Scotty looked at him suspiciously. "You do?"

"I do."

They went along in silence for a while, then, Scotty said, "But that book room of yours – the one I shot the glass roof out of – now *that* was quite a place."

"You liked my library? I hated it. I sat there for too many wasted hours."

"I never been one for reading much. But the sight of all them books in one place. Hmmm. They say books do something religious for a man's soul. And I can believe that."

Johnson wiped the sweat from his eyes. "You know what? Out of all those books – all the classics and all the literature – the ones I enjoyed the best were dime cowboy novels."

"That's 'cuz you got honest taste, Johnson," Scotty told him. "Honest taste."

"You know, I never told anyone that before."

Scotty Laughed. "What's the matter? Scared people would laugh at you?"

Johnson laughed too, "I guess I was, at that.

Scotty cleared away the dust from the top of one of what he called his tin-can springs while Johnson looked on. The top was unscrewed and Scotty's dipper was inserted into the hole. Out came pure, cool water. Scotty poured it into Windy's bowl and as the dog lapped, he drew another measure for Johnson and poured it into his old cracked porcelain cup.

When Johnson tasted it he put his head to one side and then announced knowingly, "An elegant and complex nose with petroleum notes and hints of kerosene. Crisp with a lasting impression of sump oil, but still quite supple on the finish."

"Nothing like a drink of water when a man's thirsty."

"You know what? There's not a fine wine in my cellar, and probably the world, that could compete with this right now."

Scotty gave him a long look. "Albert, I do believe you're getting into the correct way of thinking at last."

"You think."

"Oh, yes." Scotty poured himself a measure and added, "I do."

As Scotty sipped, Johnson took out his map and opened it out. "So how far is it to the Peerless Mine now?"

"Oh, quite a ways yet."

Johnson eyed Scotty as he drank. Scotty wiped his mouth and, just as Johnson had foreseen, he changed the subject. "They can keep all their fancy beers and soda pops. They ain't desert drinks. There's nothing like plain water for an actual thirst. And that's Death Valley Scotty telling you."

"You drink some pretty fancy drinks in Los Angeles," Johnson observed wryly.

"Ah, but that's city living. The purpose of booze is to make sure a person leaves a room a whole lot happier than when he went into it. But out here there ain't no rooms." He sighed an immaterial sigh. "Albert, I hate to say it, but I can see I'm going to have to teach you how to have fun when we get back to town."

Johnson looked down at the tin-can spring.

"This is a pretty nice idea."

"Well, it ought to be. I'm a pretty nice feller."

"And modest too."

"Oh, Yeah. And that. I see you've noticed at last."

The afternoon sun went down and down as afternoon suns always do. A spangling of stars emerged from a gloaming of unpaintable colors. The constellation of the Scorpion twinkling in bright points in the south, the Milky Way dusting the dark eastern sky and, like a violet diamond on a ring in the west, brilliant Venus.

Later, as the full majesty of night settled over them, Scotty lit them a fire. He and Johnson camped out with the coyote's howl and the jack asses stamping about, keeping the snakes away. Up popped the full moon, round and yellow and bigger than Johnson had ever seen it, and as it climbed higher everything below was lit by its lambent light.

Two earthmen were happily eating sausages hot from Scotty's skillet.

"How far is it to where we're going now?" Johnson asked.

"I can't tell you in miles."

Johnson tried again. "Well, how far is it in hours?"

110

"Can't tell you that neither."

"Well, what *can* you tell me?"

Scotty sat back. "Relax. Have faith. Tell me what you think of the sausages."

Johnson fell silent, but he was watching Scotty all the time, judging him.

"There really are rattlesnakes out here, aren't there?" Johnson said uneasily after a while.

Scotty took his eyes off the moon. "All kinds of snakes. More than you can shake a stick at."

"You know. I haven't seen one."

"That's 'cuz they only come out at night."

"But I've never seen them at night either."

"They don't like company much. They can feel the jacks stamping their hooves. Vibrations make them clear out. What do you think of the sausages?"

"They're good. As a matter of fact, they're *very* good."

"How's your back."

"Sore. But ... in a good way."

Another silence descended.

It lasted until Johnson sighed. He had been staring up at the heavens. "Look at that. Doesn't it just make you wonder what it's all about?"

Scotty stared too. "Nope."

Johnson looked at him questioningly. "Come on! You'd have to have the soul of a rock not to wonder at the way the night sky looks from here."

"See, Albert, it's like this: I never wonder what it's all about because I already *know* what it's all about."

Johnson showed that he was unconvinced. "Oh, you do, huh?"

"I been most everywhere in this nation. Been most everywhere across in Europe, too. And everywhere I went I asked every wise person I met that same great big question."

It might have been the fire, it might have been the sky, it might have been a twinkling in Scotty's eye, but curiously, Johnson's lack of conviction began to fade.

"And what question was that?"

"'What's the meaning of life?' I used to ask that a lot, and you

111

know what? I never did find out. Not until last month anyhow."

"What happened last month?"

"See, a couple of years back I done this favor for Bob Peg Leg – he's an old Paiute Indian friend of mine."

"I think I remember him."

"Yeah, well. He told me about this here medicine man, name of To-lo-a-che. Straight out one night Bob says to me, 'To-lo-a-che knows the answer to your question.' So ever since then I been trying to find him."

Johnson laughed gently. "Aw, go on ..."

"Listen, Albert – why do you think I want to come out here all the time? It ain't for gold. Got enough of that. Nope. Every spare moment I got since I spoke with Bob Peg Leg I spent in looking for that ol' medicine man, and last week – I found him."

"You did?"

"Uh-huh. Right up there in the Grapevines, setting all alone outside of a cave, he was, just watching the sun go down over Telescope Peak."

"So ... what did he say?"

Scotty watched Johnson for a moment. He was thoughtful. "If I told you that, Albert, then you'd know too."

Johnson's voice was real gentle now. "Aw, Scotty. You can tell me. What did he say?"

"You'll just laugh if I tell you."

Johnson felt the peace of the night penetrate through to his bones. "Scotty, I think we've been through that."

"Well ... all right. See, I sets me right down there in front of him. And he looks at me like he's been putting down a little too much of that jimsonweed whisky them boys drink. Anyways, I tells him how long I been on his trail, and how for all of my natural days I been searching for the answer to the big question, 'What is the meaning of life?'"

Albert Johnson put his head back and closed his eyes, but he was listening closely.

"Well, he just nods real slow and says, 'Ah! The meaning of life!' and lets out this long, low sigh. It was the saddest sound I ever heard come out of a living man."

Johnson shook his head fractionally, but it was not in disbelief.

112

His imagination had been fired up. "What did he say?"

"To-lo-a-che he says to me. 'I cannot tell a white man.' But then he looks me in the eye and says, 'But, my friend you are no ordinary white man, you're a true friend of the desert, and therefore I will vouchsafe to you my wisdom.' Scotty paused, and then went on. "So, I'm listening to this and waiting on his every word, and he sighs and says to me, 'The answer to your question, my son, is ... blueberry cheesecake.'"

Johnson opened his eyes with a jolt.

"Blueberry cheesecake?"

"That's what To-lo-a-che said. And you can bet I'm right riled up to hear this 'cuz I'd rid a long way and climbed over a lot of hot rock to get to that cave. And you can be sure I was not pleased to hear his answer. And I says to him, 'To-lo-a-che, you are one ol' faking sonofabitch. You mean to tell me I come searching after you for two years and more and you have the 'frontery to tell me that the secret of life is blueberry goddamned cheesecake?'"

Johnson was spellbound.

Scotty said: "And his jaw just drops down and starts quivering and he says to me, "You mean ... you mean ... it's *not* blueberry cheesecake?"

They got up with the sun next morning. They struck camp and loaded up under the light of a superb sunrise. The air was like velvet. Scotty shaved with the water from his canteen, a mirror hooked to the side of his best mule. He was soaped up and using his trusty cut-throat razor when Johnson came up tying his necktie.

"What day are you due to appear in court in San Bernardino?"

"Six days' time."

"Tuesday?"

"Yup."

Johnson absorbed the information like a piece of blotting paper and then nodded thoughtfully. "And your brother's going to testify against you?"

Scotty's head was held chin up. He was scraping the razor up the left side of his throat. "I am ashamed to admit it, but yup."

"That's hard to bear."

There was a momentary hesitancy with the razor, then Scotty

continued scraping.

"He's been put up to it by them ringtail lawyers."

Johnson considered for another moment, then said, "Listen, I've been thinking it over. Maybe we should turn around and go back."

Scotty's razor stopped in mid shave.

"What?"

"I'm serious. I'd like us to turn around and go back. I have a business to run back in Chicago, and you have to be in Court. It makes no sense for us to keep on like this."

Scotty looked directly at him. "I thought you wanted to see the mine with your own eyes."

"What's wrong with *your* eyes?"

"Nothing."

"Well, we both know what you've seen with them."

"Do we?"

"Let's turn around."

Scotty's eyes followed Johnson's every move. "I thought you liked it out here."

"I do."

"But you don't want to look at the mine?"

"What would be the point?" Johnson offered a mysterious smile. "I think I've found what I came looking for. Haven't I?"

Some hours later they were riding up Wingate Pass, rising up out of the Valley. It had been right around here that Warner had been shot. Pretty soon they came to a neat pile of rocks. There was a pole stuck in it and a sign that said:

WINGATE PASS (ELEVATION 1,976 FT)

SAN BERNARDINO COUNTY / INYO COUNTY

Scotty whoa-ed his mule. "Just a minute."

"What's the matter?" Johnson said.

"Want to give me a hand with something, Albert?"

"Sure."

Scotty looked away off across the trail with its incline up to the left. Then he approached the rock pile and began to haul on the pole until it came free.

"Help me with this."

Scotty and Johnson, carried the sign a couple of hundred feet down the track. Then, for the next hour, they labored to shift the rock pile to a new location. Johnson held the pole straight while Scotty placed the rocks just so around its base. He placed rock after rock, and then, when he had got it looking exactly like it had been before, he dusted off his hands. Then he stepped back, took off his bandana and wiped his face.

Both men looked at the sign appreciatively, then Scotty said, "That ought to do it."

Johnson said, "Not a bad job. No one would ever know."

"Warm work."

"You said it."

Scotty grinned. "Them damned ringtail lawyers think they got me whupped worse than a red-haired step-child."

As they prepared to mount up and move on again. Johnson remarked, "You said you once worked as a water boy on a survey team."

"Yup."

"What kind of a survey?"

"Oh, you know – guvvermint."

"Not a survey for drawing up and marking county boundaries, by any chance?"

"That I don't recall." Scotty shrugged. "Johnson, you know what?"

"What?"

"There are some pretty smart fellers come out of Chicago."

Johnson nodded like a man taking due praise. "One or two."

"I ought to try to remember that."

Johnson nodded again. "Yes, you ought."

CHAPTER TWENTY-THREE

Los Angeles

OUTSIDE THE HOTEL Lankershim a heap of *Los Angeles Examiners* were being slammed down on the busy sidewalk. Danny Mayer took them to his stand, cut the string bindings with his knife, picked up the paper and read. Then he shouted out excitedly just what he had read to any passer-by who he thought might be interested.

"Extra! Extra! Death Valley Scotty! Big trial collapses!"

"I'll take one of those, young feller."

The boy beamed up at his customer and took a ten dollar bill.

"Keep the change," Scotty said, and went inside the hotel lobby to read about his exploits. All in all, he had had a busy day.

The *Examiner* made excellent reading, and filled an awkward gap of time before Kate arrived from Hathaway's hat shop. He stood up and was beaming with smiles as they meet. She was overjoyed, not to say greatly relieved.

"How many times did I tell you, Kate?" he admonished. "You just got to have faith."

"But what happened? Why did the case collapse?"

"What you call one of them there legal technicalities."

"I see. So ... they didn't find you innocent?"

"Law courts ain't there to find folks innocent, only not guilty."

"I'm so pleased they let you go."

"They had to. The alleged crime turned out to be outside of their jurisdiction."

Kate looked nonplussed. "I don't understand."

Scotty grinned. "My lawyer introduced an expert witness by the name of Duke Salinger."

"Expert in what?"

"He's a surveyor. He testified that the shooting happened 100 yards north of the San Bernardino-Inyo County line. And – viola! No more case."

"Viola?"

"It's what the French say, ain't it?"

"I think you mean 'voila!' A viola's a kind of big fiddle."

"Well, so was the case against me, so that's perfect. And an end to all the calumnies."

Kate closed in on him, hugged and kissed him. "I'm glad it's over. Promise me you'll quieten down now. That we'll start living a normal life."

Scotty kissed her on the cheek and set her down. "This *is* my normal life, Kate. I don't know how to do nothing else."

As they broke their clinch Scotty folder the newspaper and handed it to a passing stranger.

"Want to read some real good news?"

The stranger acknowledged the gift with a touch of his hat brim and walked on.

Kate said, serious now, "I want you to promise me: no more lawyers. And no more newspaper men. Please."

Scotty's eye strayed nostalgically towards the bar. "I learned something, Kate: there's only two things lawyers are real good for, and one of them's scooping out a man's wallet real quick."

"And the other?"

"Drumming up publicity. There's nothing like a good old trial to get all the wolves thinking they can smell a man's blood."

"I was so worried for you."

"Ah, worry never does a body any good. The way I live, if I worried at all I'd be worried to death."

"Well, then, now you know how I feel all the time. I can't live like this anymore."

"Come on, Kate. Now you ain't gonna start blubbing on my account, now? Not with this being one of the happiest days of my life?" Scotty wiped away a tear from her eye. "Faith! Remember? And now I'm gonna spend my last twenty bucks on dinner."

The big Moorish dome of the La Grande depot Santa Fe station rose above the street like a mosque. A delicious aroma filtered across from the kitchens of the Harvey House restaurant where Scotty and Johnson had just had a bite to eat.

Johnson was tanned and healthy looking as he stood now with Scotty on the platform. Judging by all the blasts of steam, a train was preparing to depart. Johnson was back in his Eastern business clothes again.

"You know," he said. "Bessie won't recognize me. I never felt so good in my whole life."

They walked down to the end of the car and Johnson boarded. He turned, and asked, "What will you do now Scotty?

"Don't you worry about me. I'll get by. I always do."

"You do, and that's a fact," Johnson said ruefully. "Give my love to Kate."

"I will."

"I guess this is where we say goodbye."

"So long, Albert," Scotty said. "It's been nice knowing you. No hard feelings about not getting up as far as the Peerless Mine, huh?"

They shook hands lingeringly, and their eyes met, man to man.

"No. There's no hard feelings," Johnson affirmed. "I guess we both learned something out there, didn't we?"

"I guess we did. You keep that spine of yours exercised now. Y'hear? Buy yourself a mule."

"I will."

The train pulled out, and Scotty watched after it until it had passed out of sight, then he pulled a paper out of his pocket. It was a final demand from the hospital for a thousand dollars. A tired expression flitted across his face, then he screwed up the paper and threw it on the ground.

Two hours later Scotty entered an eight storey building on Grande Avenue and 4th. He rode the elevator to the top floor and located a fancy office. The glass frosted panel read:

Tonopah Investment Co.

Z. Beldon Gaylord

The office was a little showy but also pretty sparse, and Scotty though it looked like a place where not all that much actual office work got done. Gaylord, he knew, relied on 'deals.'

"Well, you'd better sit down," Gaylord said, indicating a chair on the far side of the big desk.

Scotty went instead to look out the window, arms folded and head tilted over in a characteristic pose. He was thoughtful, subdued

118

even.

"So ... how's your brother?"

"Won't speak to me."

"No?"

"Says he won't ever speak to me again. Damned ringtail lawyers filled his head with lies."

Gaylord watches him for a moment, saying nothing.

Scotty heaved a sigh. "My Daddy told me when I was a boy: 'Son,' he said, 'never have nothing to do with perfessionals – especially doctors, accountants and lawyers.' Just a bunch of sheep ticks, the lot of 'em."

Gaylord sat back in his chair and put his feet up. "So, your Mr. Johnson went back East and left you high and dry."

Scotty straightened. "I won't hear nothing said against Albert Johnson. He's a good man."

"Sure," Gaylord chuckled, "but he got you all figured out, didn't he? And all because you wouldn't show him your hard-to-find gold mine. I guess he just thinks you're a loser now, so I can understand how you must feel."

"Zee, you don't know nothing."

"I know enough to do business with you."

Scotty looked at Gaylord's smile and, for some not very hard to find reason, he thought of snakes and lizards.

"Scotty, I got a proposition for you."

Scotty took the information calmly. "Better be a good one."

"Oh, it is." Gaylord waved his hands expansively. "How would you like to sit back and let someone else do all the hard work for a change?"

"I'm listening."

"How would you like to retire from the gold mining business while you're ahead?"

Scotty inclined his head. "Zee, life just ain't that simple."

But Gaylord was coiling ready to strike. "Maybe it is. See, there's one sure-fire way of making Frank Sanders put you right back on those front pages where you belong. One piece of news he won't be able to resist."

"And what's that?"

Gaylord's conspiratorial stare was enough to freeze the Los

119

Angeles river. "When you sell your gold mine."

Scotty put his head to one side and folded his arms. "What did you say?"

"Just think on it, my friend," Gaylord suggested with slitheringly persuasive earnestness. "I'm prepared to set up a company that's going to buy up every claim in Death Valley. I'm going to issue stock in that company and sell certificates to the public at a dollar a time. It's like a license to print your own money – except that it's absolutely legal. Investors will flock to us. You'll get to build that desert castle you've always dreamed about."

"You want to buy me out?"

Gaylord took his feet off the table and opened a desk drawer. "I sure do. And for a potential fortune." He slid a contract towards Scotty. "Just sign these papers right here. It'll make us partners, so that after the first million all profits will go to you and the other three original claim owners. You'll get a full half. The rest of them'll split what's left."

"A full half, eh?"

"Sure! And just to show goodwill I'll give you two hundred dollars cash."

Scotty felt like a man does when a man-trap closes on what was supposed to be his leg. "Right now?"

"Right here and now. On the nail. As signature fee."

Scotty squinted at the paper briefly, then looked up. "What's all this lawyer talk?"

Gaylord's hand made a quick flourish in the air "Just what it says. It gives our company the right to use the name 'Death Valley Scotty Mining Company.' Each share certificate will have your picture on it."

Scotty allowed himself a grin. "My picture, huh?"

"Yeah. See, people have heard of you. There's not a person in America that hasn't read about you on the front page of some newspaper or another. Your name'll give folks confidence to invest. And that's what this business is all about. Confidence."

"Two hundred dollars on the nail, you say?"

Gaylord handed him a pen. "Just think of the headline. You can see it now: 'Death Valley Scotty Sells The Peerless Gold Mine for a Million Dollars.' You'll be big news again!"

CHAPTER TWENTY-FOUR

DR CHESLEY KILGORE MD was in his garden hammock, dressed in pajamas and sleeping cap as his maid brought out an early morning tea tray along with the morning paper. Kilgore pulled his spectacles from his pocket and looked at the front page of the paper. The headline read:

DEATH VALLEY SCOTTY SELLS GOLD MINE FOR A MILLION DOLLARS

Kilgore pulled off his spectacles again. "Well now, Mr. Death Valley Scotty," he said to himself. "I do believe I've got you right where I want you."

Kilgore rolled out of his hammock and hoofed into his house to pick up the telephone.

"Hello? Operator? Give me Santa Monica 341." he said vaguely mistrusting the instrument. "Hello? Hello? Windrush? Is that you on the end of this infernal thing?"

Unintelligible Windrush noises came out of the earpiece. Kilgore ignored them and said, "What time are you in court today?"

Garble, garble.

Kilgore nodded. "Well, I'd like it if you were to drop by."

Garble, garble, garble.

"No, no. The house. Yeah. On your way to the office. It's about that crook, Scott – Uh-huh. The one who never paid me that thousand dollar fee."

Garble.

"Oh, you read it this morning? Good. Well a thousand of that million is mine and I aim to wring it out of him."

It was not long before Windrush was drawing up outside Dr. Lawton's house. By now the owner was breakfasting out on the back deck. A jug of orange juice, toast in a silver rack, all on a starched linen tablecloth. Kilgore was wearing white shirt and tie and a vest. His Lawyer Windrush was impressively professional, being dressed for the office. From time to time the serious-faced maid came to the table. Each time, she had the sense that some negotiation had gone

121

down, not entirely to Kilgore's liking.

"Windrush, I told you: I just want my money," Kilgore said testily.

"I'm afraid you won't get it, doctor."

"Windrush, if I conducted my business like you conduct yours people would be falling down dead all over the place."

Fortunately Windrush knew all about how to handle himself with diplomacy and tact. "It's not a question of my competence. I'm pretty sure Scott hasn't any sequesterable assets."

Kilgore slapped the paper. "But it's here! In black and white, godamnit! He's a millionaire!"

"Do you believe everything you read in the papers?"

"Yes ... I mean, no." Kilgore saw the pitfall in trying to answer rhetorical questions. "What do you mean?"

Windrush resumed his lawyerish air. "Here's some news that hasn't broken yet: Scott's up to his neck in a penny-ante stock swindle. I've been asked to prosecute his partner. And to make it stick I'll have to prove that the stock issue is a fabrication."

"You mean ..."

"Uh-huh."

When he had worked out the significance of that, Kilgore showed himself to be severely put out. "Well, if I'm not going to get my thousand, I want Scott to have to admit that he's a liar and a cheat. I want him to damn himself out of his own mouth and confess he's broke. I want you to grind that golden reputation of his right back into the dust where it belongs!"

In Number One courtroom at the Los Angeles County Court Scotty was standing before the judge, looking up at the white-haired old gentleman with guileless blue eyes. Kate was at his side, which was good. Windrush was a couple of paces away to their left, which was not.

"It says here there's a court order for a thousand dollars outstanding on you, Mr. Scott," the judge said. "Why didn't you pay it?"

Windrush judged his moment, plunged the knife in and readied himself to twist it. He said , "Your honor, I believe it's not that the defendant *won't* pay, it's that he *can't*. Isn't that true, Mr. Scott?"

Scotty said nothing.

Kate reacted to the insinuation by looking to Scotty to refute the lawyer. She couldn't understand why he would not.

The judge said, "Well, that's a most tolerant attitude Mr. Windrush, though not entirely in your client's interests, if you don't mind me saying so." He turned to Scotty. "Well, which is it, Mr. Scott? Won't? Or can't?"

Scotty stared back. "I won't tell you that, judge."

"Oh, yes you will," the judge said, pointing his gavel at Scotty. "Because if you take that line with me, I'll send you to jail for contempt."

As Scotty's eyes narrowed defiantly, Kate finally lost her cool and said, "Well, *say* something, Scotty!"

Scotty's jail cell was comfortable enough. To a man used to sleeping under the stars on hard ground and relying on mules to keep the place rattlesnake free, it was no hardship at all.

When Windrush turned up Scotty pushed the brim of his hat up and opened his eyes.

"Go ask Gaylord for the money," he said.

Windrush, still as sly as a weasel, said, "Why do you say that?"

Scotty opened his hands in an innocent gesture. "Because he's got all the money that ringtail quack of yours thinks he deserves. A thousand bucks for pulling a lil' ol' slug out of a man's leg – a few stitches here and there – seems a powerful amount for a half hour's doctoring."

Windrush was not to be sidetracked. "You agreed the figure. That constitutes a verbal contract."

Scotty pursed his lips. "I was flummoxed right then. I didn't know but Warner was fixing to die. He may be as dumb as a post but he's still my brother. That quack of yours could have picked himself any amount." He showed a sudden exasperation. "Go see Gaylord. He'll pay you out."

"I'm not going to see anyone. I'm here to see you."

"Fine. You don't have to. You just set right there. He'll be here with my bail money directly."

"Z. Beldon Gaylord. He's the fellow who has stood bail for you in the past, isn't that right?"

"Two five hundred dollar bonds. You can check on that all you like."

Windrush grimaced. "Well, I wouldn't count on his help this time."

"Why not?"

"Because he's skipped town. That stock issue of his is in ruins, and you – you've been left holding the sack."

Scotty put his had to one side and sat up. "Gaylord's left town? Without even telling me? I don't believe it."

"You'd better. He's gone. Like a rat quitting a sinking ship." As Windrush fingered the bars thoughtfully, Sheriff Ralphs appeared on the far side. "But you won't be going anywhere, Mr. Scott. I know that because I just bailed you out myself."

Scotty knew a curve ball when one hit him. "I'm not sure I like the sound of that."

Windrush showed a row of small, pearly teeth. "Nor should you. Because I'm going to have you rearrested on charges far bigger than a County Court contempt."

"What charges?"

"Fraud. Perpetrating a stock swindle. Grand larceny. Take your choice ... They'll probably put you away for ever!"

That night the cell was darkly lit. Scotty was sitting on the edge of his bunk, hands together, face downcast, hatless. Kate was there in tears, standing alone in the shadows of the bars, trembling.

"I told you. I can't live like this," she told him. "I just want a normal life."

Scotty's face was grave as he looked up at her.

"Stand by me, Kate," he said.

"I want to ..."

She dissolved into full sobbing, and as Scotty stood and hugged her to him, her face, hidden from him, was one of despairing regret.

CHAPTER TWENTY-FIVE

Los Angeles – Superior Court

MORNING SUNSHINE WAS streaming into the court room through tall windows, illuminating everything. Cooling fans turned dutifully overhead. Horse and auto traffic noise filtered in distantly from outside. Two hundred people were packed onto the public benches. They were listening attentively, on account of the fact that there was expected to be blood on the walls before the session was through. Despite herself, Kate was there too, looking like a woman who was fighting the last stages of nervous exhaustion.

Windrush, on the other hand, was sprightly. He was walking up and down with showy attorney sarcasm, just as lawyers like him were wont to do.

"So just where *is* all your fabled golden wealth, Mr. Scott?"

Scotty turned to the judge. "Your honor, I don't like this feller's tone of voice."

The judge almost, but not quite, rolled his eyes. His usual mien was one of patient resignation, though underneath it he was enjoying this case quite a bit. "Just answer the question, Mr. Scott."

"What was it again?" Scotty asked.

Windrush persisted. "It was: where did your *money* come from?"

Scotty sniffed and his chin jutted at a resolute angle. "I can't say. All I know is that it's a long, long way from this room right now."

The judge responded firmly. "That reply won't cut any ice here, Mr. Scott. You'll answer the questions put to you accurately and truthfully."

Windrush harped the same old harp again. "How much money has passed through your hands since you first entered Death Valley?"

"I don't know. I never did no paperwork on it."

"If the stories about you are to be believed, it must have been millions. Isn't that right?"

"The newspapers know I like to spend pretty freely when I come to town."

"Oh, yes, you spend pretty freely, all right. In fact, you are a legend of pretty free spending, aren't you?"

"No law against spending money is there?"

Windrush turned on his heel. "No law at all. So long as it's yours to spend." He let his eye pass along the front row of jurors. "So tell us – where did it all come from? All this pretty freely spent money?"

"That's already a matter of record."

"Would you care to refresh the court?"

"Nope."

"Then I will: some of it from a Mr. James Garrett. The rest from a Mr. Albert M. Johnson. That's right, isn't it?"

"You could say that."

"And who *are* these gentlemen?"

Scotty eyed Windrush with an unsparkling eye. "My partners."

"Did you say 'partners?'"

"You got something wrong with your hearing, Windrush?"

That brought a bang of the gavel from the judge. "Just answer the question."

"Yeah, I said 'partners.' They're men who grubstaked me."

Windrush turned to the judge. "They are indeed two Chicago gentlemen, your honor. And I have here a signed affidavit from one of them." He turned back to Scotty. "According to Mr. Garrett you received from him in all near ten thousand dollars, and a little over five times that figure from Mr. Johnson. Is that not so?

The Court stirred. There were gasps and whisperings. These were unimaginable sums.

Scotty said blithely. "I can't say how much it was."

Windrush stiffened and whipped round. "Excuse me?"

"I said, I never kept no records."

"You never kept no records," Windrush repeated, rubbing salt into it. "How remarkably convenient. Well, fortunately for this court, Mr. Garrett *did* keep records. He advanced you a total of nine thousand one hundred twenty-six dollars and fifty-two cents. For which money he saw not one single ounce of gold in return. Isn't that so?"

"Whatever I got I spent. I never kept none of it."

Windrush, who was a natural-born dramatist, broke into a laugh. "Oh, yes. A person would have to have been living on the planet Mars not to know that you spent it. But you spent it in the bars and

126

restaurants of Los Angeles, didn't you? And not for the purpose for which it was obtained – which is to say, gold prospecting?"

Scotty's lawyer, a Mr. Goldman by name, who had been singularly good at keeping his own counsel, thought it was high time he jumped up.

"Objection, your honor!"

The judge nodded. "I too am beginning to lose patience with this line of questioning, Mr. Windrush."

Windrush approached the judge. "My intention is to establish certain relevant facts about the accused's character and customary manner of transacting business, your honor."

"Oh, well. Objection overruled. Continue."

Windrush now turned his back on Scotty. "Isn't it true that your conspicuous spending sprees were all merely a show? A deliberate exercise designed to dupe the public into believing you were a wealthy man?"

Scotty murmured, "You could put it that way."

"Speak up Mr. Scott," Windrush insisted. "The courtroom can't quite hear you."

Scotty raised his head. "I said, you could put it that way."

Windrush closed aggressively. "Yes or no, Mr. Scott?"

Scotty locked horns with him. "Yes!"

Windrush sheered away, letting his clipped tones wash over the jury. "And the truth is, you never at any time had any money of your own."

"The most I ever had of my own money was twenty bucks," Scotty said. "There's no crime in being poor, is there?

Windrush headed off that question like a wayward steer. "No. Not at all. But if you're so poor, perhaps you'd like to explain how you were able to finance your famous train ride. It's common knowledge that you paid ten thousand dollars cash for that little transcontinental extravaganza."

"Oh, that's easy. Z. Beldon Gaylord passed me an envelope with three five thousand dollar bills in it. Two I give right back to Santa Fe, where they come from. The third I was meant to spend as loud as I could."

"So the whole stunt was the idea of the Santa Fe Railroad Company? Cheap publicity to help them win the U.S. Mail contract."

"You just said it yourself – it weren't so cheap."

Unruly elements among the public benches chuckled at that, but Windrush ignored it all and pressed on. "You fixed it all up with the Santa Fe Railroad Company? With this, this ... Z. Beldon Gaylord acting as intermediary?"

"I told you, didn't I?"

"The same Z. Beldon Gaylord who you were relying on to put up bail money for you? The same Z. Beldon Gaylord who's presently eluding the law following the collapse of the swindle which forms the basis of complaint here today?"

"I guess that's all the same feller. Not many others could get away with a name like that."

There was a moment of silence as the packed court absorbed the significance of what had been said.

"You guess that's all the same feller. Which brings us right back to the present, doesn't it? How much money did Gaylord pay you for your non-existent Death Valley mine?"

"Gaylord was a friend of mine -"

"I asked you how much he paid you! The jury needs an answer, Mr. Scott!"

Scotty fidgeted. "He paid me two hundred dollars signature fee. For my name and my picture."

"Two – Hundred – Dollars. Thank you, Mr. Scott, for precisely valuing yourself for us." He closed in for the kill. " "There never was any Death Valley gold mine, was there?"

"I guess not."

The unease in the court rose, then responded to the sound of the Judge's gavel.

Scotty said, "Truth is I never dug no hole. And I never took out no gold. If that's what you want me to say."

Kate, who had been watching all along finally lost her composure. In tears she got up, struggled past a row of people and ran out up the aisle towards the exit.

More unease afflicted the court. And more gavel.

Windrush was savoring his victory. "No further questions, your honor."

The judge looked over his glasses pleased to hear that the

contending parties had wrapped up the morning session in good time for lunch.

"You may step down." He banged his gavel. "Recess for lunch. Back at two thirty."

Out in the courthouse lobby Kate was in tears and metaphorically beating on Scotty's chest.

"How could you have done this to me?"

Scotty metaphorically wrestled with her, embarrassed as people watched. "Kate – you don't understand -"

"You *lied* to me! You promised you were for real, but you lied to my face. How could you do that?"

Scotty tried to be humble and contrite, a role he had never been built for. "It wasn't like that? Don't you see?"

"It took a court of law to get it out of you." She paused, speechless at the enormity. "I don't ever want to see you again."

Scotty found himself triggered by the threat. "Oh, that's fine! You wanted me right enough when you thought I was rich!"

It was a stupid thing to say. stupid and unjust and beside the point entirely. He knew it as soon as he said it, but the wicked little cat was out of the bag. Kate stared at him as if the enormity had just doubled, then she slapped his face.

"I *never* was interested your money. But honesty – that's everything to me!"

Scotty pleaded. "Kate, I never hurt a soul! I never would. Never."

Kate's eyes were hard on him now. "Well, you hurt mine. Goodbye, Scotty."

She turned and marched off. He went after her, but whereas the policemen on the courthouse door let her through, they would not allow a defendant to pass.

As the tall doors closed, Scotty called out, "Kate! Kate! Please don't do this!"

A little before half past two, Scotty was back in his seat. Anyone who looked closely at him would have been able to see that he had changed. He was not the man he had been a couple of hours before. Hurt was written all over his face. Scotty's lawyer, Goldman, was sitting next to him with a look all his own. He leaned over to whisper.

"Come on, willya? – Don't look so guilty."

Scotty tried. His face brightened fractionally, but only from the expression of a man barely coping with the hurt he was nursing to a man experiencing the lowest point of his entire life. As Goldman had said, it added up to one thing: guilty, but in this instance, Goldman's go-get-'em energy was of little help.

So Goldman, who took a pride in his work and did not much like losing, tried again. In a low but fiercely enthused voice, he said, "Scotty, have I got a surprise for you! Just watch me rip Windrush's face off."

Goldman stood up and approached the bench.

"I'd like to call witness for the defense, Albert M. Johnson."

As the Clerk of the Court said, "Call Albert M. Johnson!" Scotty turned towards the door, his face a very different one from the one it had been a couple of seconds before.

Johnson entered the courtroom and strode down the aisle, straight-backed as a soldier, to take his place on the witness stand. Integrity was written all over him.

Scotty gaped.

"Please state your full name," the Clerk of the Court said.

"Albert Mussey Johnson."

"Place your right hand on the Bible and say after me, I swear to tell the truth, the whole truth, and nothing but the truth, so help me God."

"I swear to tell the truth, the whole truth, and nothing but the truth, so help me God," Johnson said unerringly.

The expression on Scotty's face was one of sheer horror. He was stunned at Johnson's appearance. How *could* Goldman have been so stupid as to bring Johnson in? It crossed his mind to stand up, there and then, and inform the court that he was going to replace that no good ringtail lawyer of his, but he was so stunned that he seemed to have been dumbstruck into the bargain.

He just sat and watched Goldman circle a little, a thoughtful hand on his chin.

"Now ... Mr. Johnson," Goldman said, when silence settled. "Could you tell the court what line of work you're in, please?"

"Ah ... the insurance business," Johnson said. "National Life of Chicago."

"And in what capacity are you employed by that company?"

Johnson took the question face-on. "I'm not employed in any capacity, actually. I happen to own the company."

A ripple of amusement ran through the court.

Goldman smiled his boyish smile. He looked at the jurors and encouraged them to smile too. Goldman did this because Goldman was smart. He was encouraged as he saw that his attempts to play the courtroom were paying off. He knew that a warm courtroom immediately after lunch was an easy, comfortable, sleepy sort of place, a place where any lawyer who knew what he was doing could win the atmosphere over with a little lively good humor.

"In that case, would you mind telling the court the net extent of your personal fortune?"

Johnson came across not only as a man of integrity, but as engagingly modest and self-effacing a man as anyone could wish for.

"Not at all," Johnson agreed. "At the last time of asking my accountants told me I was worth a little over twenty-two point four million dollars." He added. "But that was last week."

Another ripple of delight ran through the watching public.

"Last week?" Goldman said. "I don't understand."

"It was ten days ago. You see, I make interest at around ten percent per annum. So I guess by now you can add a little over sixty thousand to that figure."

Goldman tip-toed across his professional stage like a legal dancer. The tone he was striving for now was mock incredulity.

"Ha ... let me get this straight, now, Mr. Johnson. You made *sixty thousand dollars* on your capital in the last ten days? Just by leaving it in the bank?"

"It's in the form of stocks, actually, but that's about right in principle."

"So – *sixty thousand*? In ten days?"

Johnson nodded, as if the feat was no feat of his. "Yes, I guess. Each and every ten days. Up it goes by another sixty thousand. It's a lucky position to be in."

Judging by the swell of noise, the public agreed with that

sentiment.

"Lucky?" Goldman said, running a hand over the top of his head. "I guess lucky is what you are. Do you happen to know what is the average weekly wage here in Los Angeles, Mr. Johnson?"

"I'm afraid, I ... No, I can't say I do."

"Well, according to official figures the average wage in the U.S. is between $200 and $400 per year. So let's call it ten bucks a week."

"Then, I guess I'm luckier than I thought."

The public laughed out loud at that, loud enough to draw a bang of the gavel.

"Yes, Mr. Johnson," Goldman said. "Even superior court judges make less than three thousand bucks a year."

The judge banged his gavel again. This time he made it plain that Goldman was dancing on thin ice.

"Get to your point, Mr. Goldman."

"I'm sorry, your honor." He turned to Johnson again. "So, the point I'm trying to make here, is that to you – *personally* – sixty thousand dollars is not a sum of tremendous importance."

Johnson sighed and put a little thought into his answer. "To me? Personally? I – well, I can't say that exactly. In fact, I ..." In consternation he turned to the judge. "May I take a little time to explain my answer to the court in full, your honor?"

The judge looked to him graciously. "I'd be delighted if you would, Mr. Johnson."

"Thank you." He turned to speak directly to the jury. "I know that sixty thousand dollars is a lot of money. And I'm sure you've heard a great deal today about this man over here and big sums of money." He gestured toward Scotty. "But I'd be prepared to bet that not much of what's been said gets even halfway close to the truth – and that's because money isn't nearly the whole story here. This man, Walter Scott, doesn't know one iota about high finance, but he gives away things that are priceless. What he gave to me are things you just can't buy. You see, he made my dreams come true."

Not for the first time that day, Scotty's face underwent a radical change of expression. He even started to blink fast, like a man who had been deeply touched by a kind remark angled in his direction.

"Your honor, I object!" Windrush called out. "This has nothing

132

whatsoever to do with the case."

"On the contrary," Johnson said. "It has everything to do with it."

The judge pointed his gavel at the erring lawyer. "Sit down, Mr. Windrush." To Johnson he said smilingly, "Sir, you may proceed."

"Thank you, your honor. You see, ladies and gentlemen, sometimes it takes a simple man from the desert to lift a veil from a person's eyes so that, for the very first time, he can see the beauty of what God created. He showed me adventure. He gave me back my health. He took away my pain. He reminded me what true spirit was. He did all of that for me. And above all he taught me how to laugh again." He turned back to the judge. "Your honor, I don't know how you can put a dollar price on those things any more than you can put a dollar price on a man. But if I was going to have to say what Walter E. Scott was worth to the world, I would have to start the bidding way higher than sixty thousand dollars."

CHAPTER TWENTY-SIX

Death Valley

MOONLIGHT FROSTED THE alluvial fans and the beds of borax evaporites. All was silent under the haughty moon. Scotty was sitting with Johnson in remote solitude. They were camping down at the base of a bluff. It was just like old times, within a circle of firelight. Windy laying down asleep. There was good humor and jokes and hotcakes in the pan and Scotty saying, "Did I ever tell you about the time I was in England with Buffalo Bill's show? That old Queen Victoria she ups and says to me, 'Now you just did some dandy shooting, my good man. I never seen the likes of it.'"

Johnson marveled. "The Queen of England said that?"

"Word for word. Albert, now would I lie to you?"

Johnson bit into one of the hotcakes. Had he been inclined towards ultimate self-sacrifice he would have died for them. Instead he said, "Know what? I never tasted anything better than this in my entire life."

"Sure you didn't," Scotty said. "See, 'cuz I'm what they call a 'coolinory genius.'"

"Oh, is that right?"

"That is most *definitely* right. I must be, see, cuz I got my secret ingredient."

Johnson took another bite. "You do? What's your secret ingredient?"

Scotty made a gesture like he was summoning up a genie. "Viola! – like the French say – Fresh air!"

Johnson laughed.

"That's Vwa-la! A viola's a kind of bass fiddle."

"I know that." He brandished his cooking fork. "But if you want to *really* taste food, you gotta have a few sizeable lungfuls of fresh air first. That's the biggest secret."

"Quite simple."

"Sure. All the best secrets are simple." He sucked his teeth. "Only it ain't a secret no more, because I told it to you."

"Oh, it's safe with me."

"I don't doubt it. But it still ain't a secret no more. You see?"

"I think I do. And you're right."

Scotty chuckled. "I know I'm right. I'm always right. There was only one time I was ever wrong, and that's when I thought I was wrong, but I was actually right."

Johnson sighed contentedly. "Oh ... isn't this the life?"

Scotty sat back. "It surely is. And that's a fact. And that's what all them ringtails out there don't know and can never learn."

They fall silent, then Scotty got serious.

"But there's always a price ..."

Johnson, with superb timing, said, "I'm sorry that it didn't work out between you and Kate."

"Yup."

"She seemed like a sweet girl."

"Yup."

"Sweet and steady."

Scotty's sigh took in all the air around. "But she was right to go. I guess she never could take a feller like me. I guess I was all just ... too much for her." After a while he said, "I want to thank you for what you done back in the courthouse, getting me off the hook and all. That ringtail lawyer wanted to skin my hide."

"I was under oath. I just told the truth."

"I told the truth too. I never had more than twenty bucks cash of my own. And I never took one ounce of gold out of Death Valley. You know, I love this place too much for that."

Johnson watched a shooting star streak and then vanish high overhead. "It's a special place, isn't it? I never saw the like of it. Just the place for a high castle."

Scotty was instantly enthused. "Oh, yah! Since I come here as a boy with that old survey team I dreamed about that castle. Crazy, I know. But I'm like that."

Scotty stretched and got up.

"Albert, I gotta go see a man about a dog."

Johnson nodded, understanding that Scotty needed to answer a call of Nature.

Windy knew better. She got up with Scotty in that mind-reading purposeful way black and white sheep dogs have. Windy led the way ahead as Scotty went over to a gully. When he got inside he struck a match, held it up to the rock. There up on the side was a hand-print

135

Indian petro glyph. Scotty puts his hand on it. In a way, it looked like a stop sign. In a another way, it looked like the old Indian "How!" greeting that happened only in Johnson's dime westerns.

But whatever it was, Scotty took it as some sort of salute. For him, it was a link with the people who had been the guardians of this place long before he ever came near. It was also a reminder that the Indians who were once here had no use for what was in the place any more than Scotty did.

There was a momentary wind that ran down the gully. It riffled the dry pages of Jeremiah Wilson's little blue notebook which was sitting on a rock. Scotty's fingers followed along the rock wall and gave him a quiet satisfaction as his eyes took in the start of a huge vein of glittering gold.

When the narrow gully opened out there was Scotty's secret revealed: a vein of pure gold. Billows of dust were blowing over a perfect exposed reef that was six inches thick and twining right along for yards and yards. He knew it would have been worth many millions of dollars, but equally it would have meant the end of the Death Valley he had always known, and the destruction of his dreams.

When Scotty's fingers explored the reef, his eyes were touched with sadness.

"Oh, Kate." he mused. "For you, I would have took just enough out of here for a wedding ring. Why couldn't you have had faith?"

EPILOG

Grapevine Canyon, Death Valley

THE NEXT DAY SAW Scotty hopping about on a level plot of dust at the base of Grapevine Canyon, with Albert Johnson spreading out a set of blueprint plans against a convenient rock. Scotty's gestures were grandiose. He was full of himself again and talking expansively about how, together, they were going to build a real castle right here in the desert.

"We can call it Death Valley castle," Scotty said. "And there'll be a bell tower with real bells in it – and red pan-tile roofs and a shady cloister."

"A campanile," Johnson said.

"What?"

"A campanile."

"Sure, one of them too, if you want."

"It's just another name for a bell tower."

"I knew that." Scotty grinned. "And a pair of iron gates, and Bessie can have a whole chapel to herself with one of them pipe organs that plays hymns from a roll of paper, and we'll have big old easy chairs stuffed full of horsehair and a indoor fountain to keep the air cool, and fireplaces for the winter ..."

"It all sounds good to me."

"Hell, we might even dig ourselves a pool out front ... plant some shade trees ... oh, I can see it now ... can't you see it in your mind's eye, Albert? ... can't you *just see it all?*"

"Yeah, Scotty ... I can see it."

*****

ALBERT M. Johnson

1872-1948

WALTER E. SCOTT

1872-1954

DEATH VALLEY RANCH STILL STANDS TODAY. IT BELONGS TO THE U.S. PARKS SERVICE, AND IS VISITED BY 150,000 PEOPLE EVERY YEAR. IT WAS PAID FOR ENTIRELY BY ALBERT M. JOHNSON, BUT PEOPLE ALWAYS CALL IT SCOTTY'S CASTLE.

NOW YOU KNOW WHY.

I hope you enjoyed reading Death Valley Scotty. If you did, then why don't you post a review on Amazon or Goodreads?

ABOUT ROBERT CARTER

I was born in Staffordshire, near Etruria, the place made famous by Josiah Wedgwood, but was brought up in Sydney, Australia and later in Lancashire, England. I studied astrophysics at Newcastle University, where I started the student science fiction society. Writing novels has always played a part in my life, and I've tried to see the world enough to be able to write fiction with the help of personal experience.

After university, the US oil industry was booming so I went to Dallas, Texas, later on I worked on rigs in various parts of the Middle East and the war-torn heart of Africa. I was aboard the Ron Tappmeyer, a rig that blew out in the Persian Gulf, killing 19 men. It was dangerous work, but well-paid, and it took me to places that outsiders rarely see, like the Rub-al-Khali of Arabia and hard-to-reach parts of equatorial Africa.

When I left the oilfields, I spent time on travel, first to East Berlin and Warsaw, then to Moscow and Leningrad. From there I took the Trans-Siberian railway to Japan. In Hong Kong, I worked on a road survey, took tea with the heir of the last king of Upper Burma near Mandalay, and on the path to Everest base camp just happened to run into Sir Edmund Hillary. After traveling around most of India, Sri Lanka and Indonesia, I returned home and took up a job with the BBC. Four years later, I left BBC TV to write. I finally settled in London, but I still like to head off to interesting parts when time allows.

CONNECT WITH ROBERT CARTER

Email: novelrob@gmail.com
Twitter: https://twitter.com/NovelRob
Blog: http://novelcarter.blogspot.co.uk/
Website: www.novelcarter.com
Facebook: https://www.facebook.com/novelcarter
Goodreads: https://www.goodreads.com/novelrob
Amazon: https://www.amazon.com/author/novelcarter